FIRE WITH FIRE

A TANNER NOVEL - BOOK 15

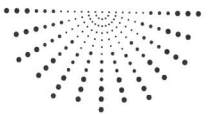

REMINGTON KANE

INTRODUCTION

FIRE WITH FIRE – A TANNER NOVEL – BOOK 15

The action heats up in the town of Killburry as the organization known as the Brotherhood attempts to take control.

ACKNOWLEDGMENTS

I write for you.

—Remington Kane

1
THERE GOES THE NEIGHBORHOOD

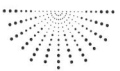

Tanner opened the front door of his home in Killburry and stepped out onto the porch with Alexa at his side. The new neighbors were going at it again, or rather, the new neighbor, as it seemed that the husband did all the yelling.

They were the McGurns, Bart and June. Bart McGurn was a big man with heavy jowls and a perpetual cigar in his mouth. His wife, June, was a petite woman with delicate features. Since the McGurns moved into the neighborhood a week earlier, Tanner had seen those delicate features with more than one bruise marring them. The bruises always appeared after Bart had one of his yelling fits.

The McGurns were getting into their car. The driveway was three houses down and to the left of Tanner's. Bart McGurn was towering over his wife and going on and on about how she should have had the cable TV hooked up by now. He kept asking her how she expected him to watch the Yankees play when the damn cable still wasn't installed.

Tanner liked baseball as much as the next man, but he

didn't think that missing a game or two was a reason to act as if the world was ending. He looked around and saw that more neighbors were coming outside to watch the show. And Tanner suspected that a show is exactly what it was.

He couldn't say why he believed that, since McGurn's anger seemed real enough. But there was just something about the way he ranted, combined with the meek way his wife, June, cowered before him. Both husband and wife would take surreptitious glances around, as if they were gauging the effect they were having on their neighbors.

"That man is an asshole," Alexa said.

"Yes," Tanner said. "He certainly seems to be, doesn't he?"

The four men that formed the neighborhood watch group began gathering near the front of Tanner's house. Two of the men lived to the right of Tanner, while the other two had homes on his left. The four huddled together as their leader, George Tucker, pointed at the bellowing Bart McGurn. They came to a decision and marched toward McGurn as one.

Being just past the dinner hour, it was too early in the day for the fearsome foursome to have donned their official neighborhood watch outfits. However, being a force of four against McGurn's one gave them a sense of courage.

Tucker disturbed McGurn in the middle of a tirade about how the dry cleaner didn't get the stain out of one of his shirts. How that could possibly be the fault of his wife, McGurn didn't elaborate on.

When McGurn spun around and saw his four neighbors, he scowled at them, then, he charged at Tucker while waving his arms and screaming at the top of his lungs.

"You four faggots better stay the hell away from me if you know what's good for you."

The neighborhood watch members retreated while making threats to call the police and spoke about McGurn disturbing the peace.

McGurn had moved closer to Tanner's home during his charge. When he saw Tanner and Alexa looking at him, he pointed at Tanner.

"What are you staring at, Myers?"

Tanner smiled. "My guess, a bit of bait perhaps?"

McGurn's look of anger receded for a moment to be replaced by a look of worry. Then, the rage came back as he gritted his teeth around his cigar and rushed toward Tanner. If he had expected Tanner to retreat like his other neighbors, he was disappointed, and soon they were standing face to face on Tanner's front porch.

"Are you trying to be smart, Myers?"

"How do you know my name?"

"What?"

"I never introduced myself to you and I doubt you sit around and gossip with the other neighbors. You spend all your time yelling at your wife."

Again, the look of worry entered McGurn's eyes. He pointed a finger at Tanner.

"Just mind your own goddamn business and we won't have a problem."

McGurn sped back down the steps and toward his car. In his absence, his wife had gotten into the passenger seat. McGurn climbed behind the wheel, started the engine, and gunned his vehicle into reverse to back out of his driveway.

As they watched their newest neighbors leave the cul-de-sac along the tree-lined road, Alexa took Tanner's hand.

"What was that you were saying before about bait? Do you think that McGurn is up to something?"

Tanner looked around again, his confrontation with

McGurn had drawn attention to him, something he didn't need. Josie Anderson was looking at him from her porch on his left, and she sent him a wink.

"The way you stood up to that loudmouth was hot, Tom. I guess we know whose is bigger, hmm? The thing I want to know is, how big?"

Tanner felt Alexa's grip on his hand grow tighter. He said, "Ignore her," to Alexa, then turned to go back into the house. After shutting the door, he smiled. "I'm not sure our new neighbor is who he seems to be."

"What do you mean?" Alexa said.

"I smell a whiff of cop scent every time I see him, and that scene in the driveway, it's just too loud, too public."

"You think he's a cop?"

"Maybe, maybe a private cop, but I also know that Chief Ellison would like to find the vigilantes operating in town. He thinks they're the neighborhood watch group."

Alexa laughed. "Maybe the chief is right, and the watch group wears ninja costumes under their bright yellow shirts."

Tanner laughed along with her. He then stepped closer and touched Alexa on the cheek.

"It's good to see you laugh. You've been down since that attack on the Burke Corporate Campus. You're worried about Deke too, aren't you?"

"Yes, I'm concerned about the infection he's developed in one of his lungs. He survived being shot three times, and now may die from a germ."

"You care about him. I knew that, but I think your feelings run deeper than you realized."

Alexa hugged Tanner. "I do care for Deke. He also saved my life before Sara saved it. If he hadn't thrown that meat cleaver, I'd be dead."

Tanner broke free of Alexa and searched her eyes. "Are you happy?"

Alexa looked confused for a moment as she seriously considered Tanner's question.

"Yes, and no. I'm happy when we're here together like this, but it fills me with dread to think that you'll be going off somewhere soon where you'll be risking your life. I do not look forward to waiting for you to return and I doubt I'll sleep well while you're gone."

"Nothing is in the works right now. Conrad Burke has enough on his hands trying to get the main building of the campus up and running again. Those neo-Nazis nearly wiped out his security force."

"Are you still going there tomorrow?"

"Yes, would you like to come along?"

"No. That building holds bad memories for me. I thought I was done with killing, but I was pulled right back into it."

"I did ask you to wait in the Jeep, and I wished that you had. Thank God Blake arrived in time to help."

"Don't you mean, Sara? I heard you call her that for the first time the other day. Have things changed between you two?"

"She saved you, Alexa. She knows what you mean to me and it would have been a fitting revenge against me to let you die."

"Oh God, I never thought of that. Was she ever that hateful toward you?"

"Possibly, in the past. But now I see that she really has moved on, and so I'll trust her, and we can start over fresh."

"Will Sara be at Burke tomorrow?"

"Yes, why?"

"Invite her here and we'll all go out for dinner. We owe

her at least that much and it would be nice to look at someone who isn't a neighbor."

"Yeah, living on a cul-de-sac is a little stifling. The only traffic we seem to get are people making a wrong turn as they head for the park."

"Why don't we go to the park? I feel like walking," Alexa said.

"All right, we'll do a bit of people watching too."

"Just don't watch that Josie Anderson."

"She's a little hard to miss, and our next-door neighbor."

"If she keeps coming on to you, I won't miss, I can promise you that."

Tanner and Alexa headed toward the rear of their house, where they could pass through a gate in their yard and enter the park.

2

UNCLE MIKE

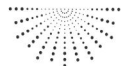

Not everyone had such easy access to a park as Tanner and Alexa.

Burt Hodges had driven to Riverside Park in Hartford from his home in Killburry. He was there to talk to his Uncle Mike. Mike Hodges had been partners with Hodges' father back when they ran a small, but highly profitable, criminal empire in Killburry.

Mike Hodges had gone away for fourteen years on a murder charge stemming from an incident in a bar fight. Mike had left prison an older and wiser man and had vowed to his daughter that he would stay clean.

Because of that, Burt Hodges had lost touch with his uncle, but he remembered the man his uncle was, and knew that his Uncle Mike was a killer at heart. Burt thought he might have need of a killer since he was risking all to gain much more.

Choa's cousin, Adán, had called and said that a member of the Brotherhood's ruling council would come to Killburry to see the properties that Hodges owned. If they were acceptable, they would hammer out a deal.

Hodges reminded Adán that the only deal he wanted would include giving him a seat on the Brotherhood's council. Adán said that he understood and had relayed that. Everything would depend on what the council member, a Mr. Chang, said at the meeting.

If things went well and Hodges forged an alliance with the Brotherhood, there would be no worries, but if they double-crossed him, he would want revenge. His Uncle Mike would dish out that revenge, or so he hoped.

He had arrived in Hartford later than he thought he would and found that his uncle had taken the grandkids to the park. Burt's cousin, Sheila, had a boy and a girl. The boy was twelve, while the girl was nine.

Hodges spotted the kids running around near the lake and looking up at the sky. He only recognized them because he had just seen pictures of the two. Sheila had spoken to him for a few minutes while he was at the house and there had been photos of the kids in the room.

The children were gazing up at the sky. An old man sitting on a nearby bench was using a controller to direct a toy drone.

Hodges followed the children's gaze and was surprised by how high the drone was. The old man had a deft touch. He was making the drone do maneuvers and zoom around. Then, the drone dived and came straight at Hodges. It lost altitude at such a fast rate that Hodges had little time to react. He soon found himself looking at the buzzing toy that hovered only a few feet away from him.

Hodges turned his head to speak to the old man and ask him what was up, and that was when he realized that the old man sitting on the bench was his Uncle Mike.

Fuck, he got old, Hodges thought, as his Uncle Mike gave him a wink.

Mike sent the drone soaring up high, then he handed the remote control to the boy.

"You got it, Jack?" Mike asked.

The little boy grinned.

"Yeah, I know how to do it. I just still have trouble landing it."

"Well, you keep it up there while I go talk to your cousin."

The little girl pointed at Burt Hodges. "He can't be our cousin, Grandpa; he's too old."

Mike laughed. "He's still your cousin, sweetie. Now stay close to your brother; Grandpa will be right over here on the other bench."

Hodges greeted his Uncle Mike with a handshake followed by a hug. The hug was shocking, as it revealed how thin and fragile the old man felt. Hodges figured that his uncle couldn't be more than sixty-five or so, but he looked ten years older. His wrinkled face brought to Hodges' mind memories of his grandfather, who died while Hodges was still a kid.

"How's Dexter doing, Burt? I haven't seen that boy since he was about the same age that Jack over there is now."

"He's okay, but I have to keep him in line."

"He sounds like you when you were a kid," Mike said, then he studied his nephew. "So, what's with the visit?"

Hodges was going to lie and say that he got to thinking about the family and decided to touch base. He scratched that idea as he looked into his Uncle's eyes and saw that Uncle Mike was still there, he was just covered in old.

"It's about this group calling themselves the Brotherhood, Uncle Mike. They're up and comers and I'm thinking of joining them."

"I take it that this group is not a Christian organization, despite what the name might suggest."

Hodges grinned as he took a seat on the bench beside his uncle. "Ah, not exactly, no."

"Burt, I don't know why you came to see me, but I'm going to give you some advice. Stay away from this Brotherhood gang and keep your nose clean. Believe me, boy, you do not want to spend your life rotting away in a cell like I did. You sure as hell don't want that for Dexter."

Hodges leaned in and whispered. "If this works out, I'll be somebody, the way my dad was. Uncle Mike, I'm so damn sick of being nobody. That's what I don't want for Dexter."

Mike sighed. "I gave you my opinion, but why did you come to see—" Mike stopped talking as he noticed that Jack was attempting to land the drone. The red and white miniature aircraft had four propellers, as well as an onboard camera that allowed its operator to have an aerial view of their surroundings.

Young Jack had crashed the drone once before while attempting to land it, which was why Mike had told him to just keep it in the air. But, instead of yelling at the boy for disobeying, Mike just observed. When the drone landed in the grass smoothly, he began clapping.

"That a boy, Jack. See, you got the hang of it. Now take her back up."

The drone rose smoothly, and Hodges and his uncle watched it ascend skyward.

"Those things are cool," Hodges said. "I would buy Dexter one, but I'm trying to get him to grow up and learn to run things, not play with toys."

"Is that why you're here, Burt, to tell me what a big shot you're going to be?"

"No, that's not why I'm here. I came here to see my Uncle Mike; the toughest man I ever knew."

"Hah! Oh Burt, that dude is dead. He had the toughness beaten out of him by prison guards and the other inmates. All I want now is to be Grandpa to those two kids over there."

"Yeah, I can see that, but I thought I could use you as a last resort."

"A last resort? I don't get it."

"The Brotherhood might play rough with me and... I might not make it. There's also a guy named Tom Myers who's connected to New York and Joe Pullo. He and I might tangle too."

Mike smiled. "Joe Pullo? Wow, there's a name I haven't heard in years. Is he running things now?"

"Hell yeah, he runs New York, at least he does until the Brotherhood heads his way."

"I'm not surprised that Pullo is top dog. Back when your father and I had that dust-up with Sam Giacconi, we had a meet with him and a couple of his men. It shocked the crap out of me when I saw Pullo. He was just a kid, no older than Dexter and maybe even younger, but you could tell that he was no boy, you know? Anyway, Giacconi and your father didn't get along see, and it looked like the shit was gonna hit the fan."

"What happened? I never heard this story."

"Giacconi had a fat guy with him, um Rossi? No, Rossetti, Al Rossetti. He and I were eyeing each other, then I see him go for his gun. All of a sudden, Joe Pullo grabbed Rossetti's wrist and shook his head, telling Rossetti to cool it. Then, Pullo started talking to your father, you know, to calm things down. Twenty minutes later, we had a deal in place, and everybody got to go home in one piece. If not for Pullo, I don't know what would have happened. So yeah, I'm not surprised that he's sitting at the top of the heap."

"He's got a man in Killburry, this Tom Myers, but I don't know why. Myers already had a run-in with Dexter and broke his wrist."

"He did what to my nephew?" Mike asked.

Hodges leaned back a little. Mike's voice had suddenly become icy and sounded young. Yeah, there was still some of the real Uncle Mike inside the old man.

"Dexter did something stupid, Myers caught him, and then he broke his wrist when Dexter pulled a knife on him. But never mind that; I'll handle that. What I want to know is that you'll get payback for me if the Brotherhood whacks me."

"Burt, don't get involved with these guys. You're already somebody. You're my nephew, and I miss seeing you. Why not leave Killburry and move to Hartford? You've got family here and I'd love to see Dexter again. That kid always reminded me of your father."

Hodges stood.

"It's too late, Uncle Mike, but listen, if anything happens to me, I want you to look out for Dexter." Hodges reached into his front pocket and took out a thick sealed envelope that contained cash. He handed it to his uncle. "That's fifty grand. If my bet on the Brotherhood goes sideways, Dexter will know to come see you, and that you'll take care of him."

Mike looked down at the envelope. "I don't want this, Burt."

"You're the only family I got Uncle Mike."

"There's your Cousin Sheila and those kids over there."

"Sheila wouldn't understand this."

"No, she wouldn't, but that's not what I was talking about," Mike said.

Mike stood and stuffed the envelope into an inside pocket of his jacket. Hodges made a face at the jacket. It was a warm spring day, and yet, his Uncle Mike felt the need to put on a jacket. It was one more thing that signaled the man had grown old.

Hodges hugged his uncle again, waved goodbye to his young cousins, and headed back to his car. In a few days, he would either come back to see his uncle with a smile on his face, or he'd be taking a dirt nap somewhere. There was no middle ground.

THERE WERE OTHER RESIDENTS OF KILLBURRY IN HARTFORD. They were Killburry's Chief of Police John Ellison, along with the security chief from Silicon City, Jim Brett, and Brett's wife, Sue. Sue and Jim went by other names as well. On the cul-de-sac they lived on, they were known as Bart and June McGurn.

Chief Ellison rubbed a hand over his chin. "Tom Myers is on to you two?"

"I don't know for sure," Brett said. "But he made a crack about me setting bait."

"Bait? That sounds like he's got your number."

"Jim slipped, too," Sue Brett said. "He called Myers by name, and we were never introduced."

The Chief chuckled. "I did peg Myers as a bright one. Now, the question is, does he have a big mouth?"

"You think he knows who the vigilantes are?"

"It's the watch group," Ellison said.

Brett laughed. "No way, those guys are just using that as an excuse to hang out together. They're not the ones committing the assaults and making the threats. I'd bet on that."

"You may be right, Jim, but there's a reason I suspect them. One of the people assaulted by the vigilantes was a man who had DUI convictions, Driving Under the Influence. When he moved to Gentry Court, that neighborhood watch group harassed him over his drunk driving record, or so he claimed. He also said that he hadn't had a drink in years."

"If he was no longer drinking then how did they know he was a former drunk driver?" Brett asked.

The chief made a face. "He drank. I verified that with a bartender in town. I think he drove into that cul-de-sac drunk as a skunk one night and that neighborhood watch group spotted him. He was later beaten, threatened, and told to leave Gentry Court or else. He moved his family out the next day and sold his house at a loss. He was also warned to keep quiet, but after a while, he contacted me and told me his story. Since then, I've uncovered several others who were similarly threatened."

"Okay, maybe it is those four guys in the watch group, and they've been playing dumb. But what's our next move?" Brett said.

"Here's what you do; turn it up a notch. When you go back to Gentry Court, wait until it's good and late and then wake up the neighborhood. Make it sound like you're practically killing Sue here. Then Sue, I'll send an ambulance by for you. Unless things are crazy tonight, I should be able to keep one on standby."

"An ambulance?" Sue said. "Why, did 'Big Bad Bart' finally go too far?"

"That's right, so go heavy on the makeup, and pretend to have a broken arm. If that doesn't make the vigilantes take action, then I don't know what will."

"Great, once the ambulance takes Sue away, I'll be a sitting duck," Brett said.

"You won't be alone; my daughter and I will be on duty and in the woods across from the houses. Plus, you are armed, aren't you?"

"Hell yeah, a Colt Python. I'll be ready for anything."

"All right then, that's the plan," Ellison said.

"Chief," Sue said. "Why did you ask Silicon City to help you with this instead of using your own people?"

"It wasn't my idea. Your CEO suggested it, and I agreed. It seems one of the sex offenders that the vigilantes roughed up and scared away was his younger brother."

Sue looked shocked. "Martin Anders brother is a sex offender?"

"He's in the registry, but he's no sex offender. I looked into it. Years ago, the CEO's brother was hiking in the woods and had to urinate, and of course, he went. Before he could zip up, a family of four appeared through the trees and saw him. They had a little girl with them and so they overreacted. Technically, the young man had exposed himself in public. Your CEO, Anders, he said he was there and whizzing on another tree. If the family had come from that direction, it might be his name on the sex offenders' registry."

"All right, so it was an accident. Why is Anders brother listed as a sex offender?" Sue said.

"According to the officer that investigated the incident, Anders brother angered the judge repeatedly. The kid was outraged at being harassed just because he took a whiz in the woods. I don't blame him, but he did himself no good when he made the judge angry. The officer told me that the judge was a bastard. He had him arrest the kid and now the young man is in the registry."

"Do you believe that's what happened?" Brett said.

"It sounds plausible to me, and the cop I talked to had no reason to lie," the chief said. "Anyway, Silicon City offered me help and I took it, now it's up to you two to deliver."

Sue slapped her husband on the face playfully. "This big bully here will put on a good show, don't worry, and I'll make them think he's a wife beating beast."

Chief Ellison smiled. "That should bring out the vigilantes. When it does, I'll move in for the kill."

3

THE MONSTER IN THE CLOSET

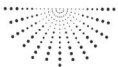

THE SCREAM WOKE TANNER AND HE SAT UP IN BED. ALEXA stirred beside him, as the sound of something heavy falling echoed in the night.

Then came a voice, the voice of Bart McGurn. It was faint given the distance between their homes, but distinct, and he was yelling something about baseball.

Tanner got dressed, as he did so, Alexa put a light on, rose from the bed, and donned a pair of shorts and a T-shirt.

"Oh my God, Tanner. It sounds like he's killing her. Are you certain that Bart McGurn isn't what he seems to be?"

Tanner kissed her. "I'm going to find out. Please stay here and I'll be back within an hour."

"An hour? Why so long?"

"I don't know how long this might take, but if you come looking for me, then the neighbors will know that I left the house."

Another scream came from the McGurns, but this one

was more a cry of pain. Alexa watched as Tanner armed himself.

"You would kill him if he's hurting her?"

"I'll likely just give him a taste of what he's dishing out."

"Be careful, please?"

"I will."

Tanner left his house by the side door after disabling the home's alarm. He was dressed totally in black and wore a night-vision monocular. After activating the monocular, he headed toward the McGurns' house.

He didn't get very far before realizing that he was not the only one prowling the night. There was a figure ahead of him in the Anderson's yard. It was a lithe figure that moved with the grace of a dancer. When a sound came from behind, Tanner took concealment at the side of a storage shed, and watched, as a second figure moved past him to join the first.

Tanner stayed with them and saw two more figures. The sounds coming from the McGurns had grown quiet, but now there was a new sound. An ambulance was approaching.

The four figures moved toward the front of the home they were at and lowered themselves to the ground behind a short row of bushes. Masked, and dressed in black, they were for all intents, invisible.

Tanner had taken position behind a tree and had a good view of the street. With the ambulance lighting up the night, Tanner had been about to power down the monocular. But then he detected two figures out in the woods.

He couldn't make out much detail, but they were both wearing uniforms and one of them had a pair of binoculars. The one with the binoculars was clearly female, and a shapely one at that.

Tanner smiled. The four figures in front of him were about to walk into a trap. June McGurn came out of her house whimpering. Her face looked not only bruised, but also bloody. She moved stiffly and was cradling one arm with the other.

The ambulance attendants ran to meet June, as behind her, Bart McGurn kept saying that his wife fell down the stairs, and that she was always hurting herself.

June was helped into the ambulance for treatment, as Tanner crouched low and moved back toward the rear of the McGurn property. He used the monocular to look for more cops but saw nothing other than two deer and a raccoon moving about in the dark. It looked as if the sting operation was being run with few people.

Tanner removed the monocular and knocked on the home's rear door. The house was set-up much like his own, with a rear deck and sliding glass doors. His knock was loud enough to be heard inside, but not thunderous enough to carry out to the street where Bart McGurn, or whoever he was, pretended to be a wife beater.

Tanner entered the house after gaining access through the sliding glass doors by picking the lock. He then moved silently through the rooms, while stopping to gather items he figured would come in useful.

There was a Colt Python sitting on the coffee table, as outside, Bart was telling the ambulance driver that he would come to the hospital later. He said he needed his sleep and wasn't going to stay up all night just because his wife was clumsy. As McGurn spoke, Tanner removed the bullets from the Colt and took concealment.

The ambulance left a short time later and Bart

McGurn came back into the house. After turning off the lights and grabbing his gun, McGurn made a call.

"I guess you watched the show, Chief. Did you see any signs of uninvited guests?"

In his hiding place, Tanner realized he'd been right about McGurn, and apparently, McGurn was working with Chief Ellison to draw the vigilantes into a trap. McGurn told the chief that he would go up into his bedroom and hide in the closet.

Before doing so, he would arrange the bed to make it look like he was asleep in it. If anyone made a move, McGurn would send a text. Once the message was sent that the vigilantes were in the house, McGurn, along with the chief and the female deputy, would take down the vigilantes.

Tanner was able to move up the stairs without being seen by McGurn. After entering the bedroom, he concealed himself again and waited.

McGurn arrived in the bedroom only a few moments later. As he said he would, he arranged the bedding and pillows so that it appeared that someone was sleeping beneath the covers. He then did something that Tanner thought was a nice touch.

McGurn placed a tape recorder in the bed. It was playing a recording of someone snoring, and it sounded realistic.

With his trap set, McGurn opened the closet door and stepped inside to wait for a visitor. He didn't realize he wasn't alone in the closet until Tanner placed a choke hold on him from behind.

McGurn attempted to struggle free, then became desperate. He bent his arm and pressed his gun against Tanner's head. Through the green glow of the monocular,

Tanner verified by sight that the gun's chambers were still empty.

McGurn pulled the trigger and the weapon *Click, Click, Click, Click, Clicked* uselessly, before dropping from McGurn's limp hand.

A few moments later, Tanner had McGurn on the bed. The man was gagged, immobile, and deafened by wads of cotton taped in place in his ears. Tanner had taken the cotton balls from McGurn's medicine cabinet, while the tape came from a kitchen drawer.

The other guests to the party didn't arrive until after another twenty minutes had passed. After creeping up the stairs and entering the bedroom, they moved toward the figure in the bed. All four of them were holding weighted batons, and there were military grade stun guns in holsters as well.

Before they could strike out at McGurn, Tanner revealed himself by stepping out of the closet and pointing McGurn's Colt Python at them. This time, the gun was loaded.

"Hello there."

ALEXA STAYED INSIDE THE HOUSE BUT CERTAINLY WASN'T going back to sleep. Feeling a bit hungry, she decided to make tea and indulge in a piece of lemon meringue pie. When Tanner unlocked, and then entered through the sliding deck doors, Alexa gasped when she saw that he wasn't alone.

"What's going on?"

Tanner went to her, kissed her, then gestured at their guests. "Say hello to the real neighborhood watch group."

They were the wives of the men on the neighborhood

watch, Anna, Louise, Tina, and Josie. Like Tanner, they were dressed in black.

Josie, always the flirt, used a finger to swipe a dap of the pie's fluffy topping, then licked it off seductively as she stared at Tanner.

"Alexa, I hope you're willing to share?"

"You'd better be talking about the pie," Alexa said.

Josie giggled. "What else?"

4
NICE TRY!

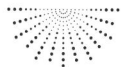

Anna Vitale smiled at the image on her phone.

The picture was coming from a camera in her home and showed her six-month-old daughter sleeping peacefully. There was also sound, and the baby mewled softly once before rubbing her little face in her sleep.

Anna then switched to a different feed, and the image of her snoring husband appeared. Her husband, Bill, was a hairy man. He was sleeping with his mouth hanging open, and a line of drool ran down his chin and onto the pillow.

As Anna checked her house, the other women were doing the same, ensuring that all was well during their absence.

"Don't your husbands realize they're being drugged?" Alexa asked.

Anna looked abashed as she answered. "We only do it once in a while, when there's a problem we have to take care of, like tonight."

"The cops nearly took care of you tonight," Tanner reminded her.

His neighbors all knew him as Tom Myers. He had told

them that his occupation was that of freelance researcher, but Anna and the other women were giving him curious looks.

"How did you know that the cops were out there in the woods," Louise Garston asked. She was a blonde with short hair. The hair had been sticking up ever since she removed her ski mask.

Tanner revealed the night-vision monocular and explained what it was.

"All right," Anna said. "That's how you saw the police, but how did you know that Bart McGurn was a phony?"

"I didn't until tonight, but he seemed to be laying it on a little thick, didn't he? I would think someone new to the neighborhood would dial their true self down, not broadcast what they are."

Josie smiled. "I think you're speaking from experience, Tom."

Tanner responded to her allegation by asking a question. "Why have none of your victims identified you all as females?"

The women laughed, then, one by one, they all spoke in what were convincing male voices. Anna also pointed out that they wore dark and baggy clothing to hide their curves.

"All right, but how long have you ladies been acting as masked avengers?"

Tina laughed, she had dark hair and wore it short, as Louise did. Both women had children, but Tanner thought you couldn't tell it by their figures, as they were slim, but shapely.

"We're not masked avengers, Tom, Alexa. We're just a group of women who are tired of having to worry about our children. There were six known child molesters living in town when we came here, six. We just made sure that they went somewhere else."

Tanner looked at Josie. "You don't have any children; why do you do it?"

"I do it because it's fun. I'm a big fan of fun, Tom. Don't you like to have fun?"

"Who doesn't?" Tanner said.

"Then maybe the two of us can have fun together sometime."

"Dial it down, Josie," Anna said. "Look at Alexa, she's ready to strangle you."

Josie smirked at Alexa. "You might be bigger than me, Alexa, but I have more skill. I'm an expert in karate and judo."

Josie was standing in front of the counter, upon which stood a block of knives. Alexa walked over, grabbed the large carving knife from the block, and told Josie to step back.

Alexa then proceeded to put on a display of immense skill as she moved the knife around in a blur of speed. The blade went behind her back in one hand only to reappear in the other, then under a leg, past her buttocks, and back around to the front.

It was almost too fast for the eye to follow. At the end of it, she thrust forward and placed the blade beneath Josie's chin before the smaller woman could twitch.

"Tell me more about how skilled you are, Josie," Alexa said.

Josie swallowed hard and looked over at Tanner. "I think we should keep our distance from each other, Tom. No offense."

Tanner smiled. "That would be healthier... for both of us."

Chief Ellison let out a great sigh as he looked down on Bart McGurn, who was actually Silicon City's security chief, Jim Brett. Brett was tied up like a Christmas turkey.

As he took out a knife in preparation to cut off the zip ties on Brett's wrists, Ellison heard laughter and turned to see his daughter giggling.

"Deputy, this is not funny."

"I'm sorry, Dad, I mean, Chief, but look at him, and this is Silicon City's best?"

"Olivia, that's rude. I'm sorry, Brett, she didn't mean it."

The chief's daughter pointed at Brett's ears. "Not only is he blindfolded, but he can't hear us either. See? He has tape over his ears, and I bet there's something stuffed behind the tape."

"Oh," the chief said, and then laughed. "He does look funny laying there like that, doesn't he? But now let's get serious; I'm going to remove the tape from his ears, along with the blindfold."

Olivia did her best not to smile, but the corners of her mouth were still tilting at an upward angle. Once the chief had Brett free, they saw that he was one very pissed-off man.

"Those sons of bitches! One of them was lurking in my damn closet. When I backed in there to hide, he choked me out."

"Are you sure it was a choke hold?" the chief asked. "People usually recover from that quickly."

"It was a choke hold all right, and when I woke up, I was blindfolded, deafened, gagged, and bound up."

"That sounds like an expert, or someone with a heck

of a lot of experience," the chief said. "They had to move you to the bed and truss you up the way you were in less than a minute."

"How long was I like that?" Brett asked, then he looked at the bedside clock. "Oh, hell, it felt a lot longer than that."

"We came in because you failed to touch base with us at the top of the hour. It's a good thing for you that we had that protocol in place, otherwise, you might have stayed tied up all night."

Brett rubbed his wrists, as he tried to get circulation back into his hands.

"So, what do you think? Was this the vigilantes sending me a warning, or am I done for and they know it was a sting operation?"

Olivia held up the note they found on the bed beside Brett. It was written in block letters with lipstick taken from his wife's dresser. The note said: NICE TRY, COP.

"You are so busted," Olivia said, and although she fought the urge. She couldn't help but laugh.

Brett's face reddened from both anger and embarrassment. "Vigilantes my ass! This was that damn Tom Myers."

"Now, Jim, we don't know that," Chief Ellison said, but Brett had already headed for the door. He ran down the stairs and out into the night with the chief and his daughter following.

Chief Ellison was speaking to Brett, trying to calm him down, but the man was hell-bent on reaching Tom Myers' house and beating the snot out of him.

Brett pounded on Myers' door, then he rang the doorbell over and over. When the door flew open, Myers, who was Tanner, stood there with a smile on his face.

"More company? Aren't we the popular ones, and at such a late hour."

Chief Ellison looked at the group of women standing behind Myers and recognized several of them, including Myers girlfriend. The girlfriend was the only one not dressed in black and the chief felt something tickle his brain. Before he could figure out what it was, Brett's booming voice interrupted his thoughts.

"Myers, you son of a bitch, I know you're the one who did it. I'm gonna kick your ass."

The chief was about to speak when Alexa beat him to it.

"Not in my house! If so much as a lamp gets broken, I'll beat up both of you."

Tanner gestured toward the lawn. "Let's take it outside, McGurn."

The chief issued a warning. "I'll arrest you both if this doesn't stop now."

Tanner and Brett ignored him. Brett was full of fury, while Tanner looked amused. Brett threw the first punch at Tanner's head and grunted with frustration as Tanner ducked beneath it. Brett threw another punch, then another, and another. Tanner either ducked or moved aside at the last instant.

Brett wasn't slow or clumsy, he was just no match for Tanner's speed and agility. Brett's inability to land a punch on Tanner only frustrated him further, and his efforts devolved into nothing more than wild swings. By the time he missed landing a dozen blows, it had become comical, and the women began giggling, including Ellison's daughter. As for Ellison, he was watching Tanner and wondered how a "freelance researcher" could have such obvious fighting skills.

The would-be fight ended when an exhausted and

sweat-drenched Brett fell to his hands and knees on Myers' lawn. He was gasping for air between muttered curses. Meanwhile, Tom Myers had never thrown a punch, he had only ducked and dodged, and the effort hadn't winded him at all. Myers looked the same as he had when he opened his front door.

The chief walked over and helped Brett to stand, then led him toward his house. The chief's daughter was staring at Tanner in admiration, that is, until her father called to her.

"Deputy Ellison, why don't we leave these good people alone?"

"Yes," Olivia said. She turned to leave, but not before sending Tanner a smile.

5

CALLED ON THE CARPET

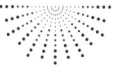

The following morning, Sara arrived at the Burke Corporate Campus and saw that there had been more changes since her previous visit.

She had been there only two days earlier and could tell that a lot had been done during that time to enhance the main building's security. There had been earlier modifications as well. Employees were no longer allowed to enter or leave through the lobby, but rather, they had to travel through a secured side entrance. Each employee would be issued a badge that not only allowed them access onto the property but would also grant them entry into the building. The badge could also be used to track an employee's location and was needed whenever anyone so much as entered a bathroom or break room.

However, there was no swiping of cards across a panel needed. All of the badge's functions were automatic. But if you arrived to work without your badge, you would not even make it onto the employee parking lot without being escorted to the building by a guard.

Sara was one of the few employees to receive a badge

so far, as many employees were still on a two-week paid furlough instituted by Conrad Burke. His people had gone through hell at the hands of a group of neo-Nazis. He was allowing them time to heal.

A few key employees continued to come in or opted to work from home. Still, the cost of the lost productivity along with the security enhancements was enormous, but Burke didn't care.

He had gone to many funerals over the past several days, as his slain security people were laid to rest. He had also given each family monetary compensation, generous monetary compensation, although, how could money ever compensate for such loss?

Sara had tossed the badge in her purse when she first received it and found it to be unobtrusive as she went about her day. However, a small smile lit her face whenever she thought of Tanner walking around the building with a badge. The image brought to mind a tiger wearing a leash.

When she spotted the new head of security, she decided to ask her if Tanner would need a badge, and if so, could she please be the one to give it to him. Sara wanted to see the look on his face.

The new head of security was familiar to Sara, as well as a recent acquaintance, and friend. Burke's new security chief was Amanda Zwicky.

Zwicky had sent Burke a memo months earlier warning him that the company's security protocols were woefully outdated and inadequate. Her memo went largely ignored, but now she was listened to and her suggestions were being implemented.

Zwicky was making three times the money she had made at Burke L.A., and Sara thought that her new friend seemed happy in her job.

"Mr. Tanner?" Zwicky said. "Yes, I understand that I'll

FIRE WITH FIRE

be meeting him later today, but he won't be coming here. Mr. Burke has other plans and has arranged to meet Mr. Tanner at a place he called, 'the lakeside property.' The meeting is scheduled to take place in forty minutes."

Sara frowned in disappointment. She so wanted to see Tanner's reaction to being told he would need to tote an employee badge around everywhere. Then, she wondered why Mr. Burke would want to meet Tanner at the lake.

"Did Mr. Burke say why he wanted to make the change?"

"No Sara, but he does want to see you in his office."

"Okay, I'll go up now."

"Sara?"

"Yes?"

"Mr. Tanner, who is he? He's not listed in any of the employee records that I have."

"It's just Tanner, not Mr. Tanner, and Tanner's job description is something that Mr. Burke will have to fill you in on."

"I see, but I did ask Mr. Burke's executive assistant about Tanner. Ella speaks highly of him. In fact, she says that he saved Mr. Burke's life, and her own."

"That's true."

"He sounds very brave. I look forward to meeting him. Mr. Burke wants me to come to the lakeside property too."

"Tanner is many things, and yes, brave is one of them."

AFTER GOING THROUGH FOUR SEPARATE SECURITY measures, which included a scan of her purse and the answering of a code word, Sara entered Mr. Burke's refurbished office. The code word changed daily and was unique to each visitor. Sara had received the code word from Zwicky before heading to the office. While she was on her way up, the guard was informed of her imminent arrival and told what code word she'd been given.

When prompted by the security guard, Sara gave him the code word that she'd received. If she had failed to give him the right word, she would never be allowed into the office.

The office's former glass wall had been replaced with ballistic glass. Inside the office, Burke's bathroom had been expanded into a section of the adjoining conference room and could now double as a safe room.

When Sara was escorted in to see Burke by Ella, she was glad that at least one thing hadn't changed. Burke still sat behind the old wooden desk that had belonged to his grandfather, the founder of the company.

Burke greeted her with a bright smile. Sara had always felt that the man liked her, but after she had saved his wife, along with Alexa, Burke seemed especially warm toward her.

"Miss Blake, how are you today?"

"I'm well, Mr. Burke, and how are you?"

Burke shook his head sadly. "I feel sick about all the people we've lost. If only I had listened to Miss Zwicky sooner."

"It would have helped, yes, but it wouldn't have stopped the attack. The police found explosives and grenade launchers inside the truck the neo-Nazis arrived in. They would have wreaked havoc one way or another. Don't blame yourself, sir."

"How can I not? Still, we have to go on, and that's partly why I want to speak with you and Tanner. We'll be leaving later to meet him at the lake property."

"Later? Miss Zwicky said that the meeting was soon."

"It's been pushed back by Tanner. He just sent me a text saying that something came up where he is."

"Oh, I wonder what that could be."

In Killburry, Tanner was riding in the rear of a police car. He wasn't cuffed or under arrest, but he had been asked to the station by Chief Ellison.

The request from the chief had been relayed to Tanner by the chief's daughter, Deputy Olivia Ellison. Deputy Ellison kept an eye on Tanner in the rear-view mirror as she drove along.

"You haven't asked why the chief wants to see you."

"No, I haven't," Tanner agreed.

"Aren't you curious?"

"It's a ten-minute ride; I'll find out when I get there."

Olivia smiled. "It involves one of your neighbors."

"You don't say?"

"Um hmm, Bart McGurn."

"The boxer?"

Olivia giggled. "I think it will be some time before he starts a fight again."

"McGurn should stick to yelling at his wife, but what about him?"

"Someone assaulted him last night. That's why he was so angry."

"He thought I had done it?"

"Yes, he did."

"Have you questioned his wife? I think she has more motive than most."

Olivia laughed. "I'll look into that, Mr. Myers."

"You do that, Deputy Ellison, you do that."

Once they were at the station, Olivia admitted to her father that she had informed Tanner about the attack on Bart McGurn.

The chief frowned at his daughter. "I wanted to inform Mr. Myers of that, Deputy."

"She couldn't help herself, Chief," Tanner said. "She was trying to get a reaction out of me."

They were in the chief's office with the door closed. Tanner sat across from the chief while Olivia stood on her father's right.

Olivia squinted at Tanner. "Why aren't you nervous? Most people would be."

"Why do you wear that uniform? Most women don't."

"I'm not most women, Mr. Myers."

"I can see that, and I'm not most men."

Olivia smiled, as a blush darkened her face. When her father turned his head and looked up at her, Olivia cleared her throat and stood straighter.

The chief sighed, then turned his attention back to Tanner.

"Do you know anything about the attack on Mr. McGurn?"

"No."

"No?"

"No."

"Would you care to elaborate on that?"

"Would I care to elaborate on, no? No, I would not."

The chief stared hard at Tanner and Tanner looked back at him with a placid expression.

"Mr. Myers, I'll be straight with you. I think you're hiding something. I think you know who these vigilantes are."

"What vigilantes?"

"You know what I'm talking about. The people who have been harassing the sex offenders, drunk drivers, and now, wife beaters."

"I thought that was your job," Tanner said.

"No, my job is to arrest those people once they're caught in the act. It is illegal to assault and threaten them. Despite their past actions, those people still have rights."

"I see, but I don't know anything about vigilantes. Perhaps you've been misinformed."

"Myers, I have statements from several people who claim to have been beaten and told to leave town."

"Are those statements from sex offenders and drunk drivers?"

"They are."

"Then, maybe that type of person is also prone to lying."

The chief pointed a finger at Tanner. "Don't try to get smart. This is serious business we're talking about here."

This time it was Tanner's turn to sigh. "This isn't serious, Chief. If what you're saying is true, it's a blessing. It would mean that you have a group of involved citizens committed to helping you and that they're willing to risk themselves to run criminals out of your town."

"My concern is that they'll one day go too far and seriously injure or kill someone."

"Someone like a child molester?"

"Maybe, or maybe someone innocent who they think is a child molester. Myers, I will not have this in my town, do you understand me?"

"I do, but as you know, I'm a recent resident. Some of these events happened before I came here."

The chief reached for a file on his desk. "About that, you seem to have appeared from thin air. I can't find anything having to do with you that goes back more than a few years. You also move around quite a bit, why is that?"

"I bore easily."

"Oh, you won't find it boring here, not if I discover that you have anything to do with the vigilantes. And Myers, do me a favor."

"Anything for you, Chief," Tanner said.

"The next time you talk to the vigilantes, let them know that I will see them prosecuted to the fullest extent."

"Am I free to go?"

"Yes."

Olivia moved around the desk to follow Tanner out, but her father called to her and made her stop.

"Have Deputy Ralston take him home. I want you to stay here. We need to talk."

"Yes, Chief," Olivia said, in a resigned tone.

She left her father's office with Tanner and handed him off to Ralston. Before he left the station, Olivia offered Tanner some advice.

"Don't do anything that would cause me to have to come get you again."

Tanner looked her over and then met her eyes as he smiled. "It might be worth it just to see you."

Olivia blushed once more, before turning and rushing back to her father's office.

6

HOLD ON

THE SOLE NEO-NAZI TO SURVIVE WAS A MAN NAMED SEAN.

Sean had been sent ahead to prepare a hideout for the group, and thus, was spared their fate. He stood among the woods that bordered the Burke Corporate Campus and watched the activity, as workers continued to make improvements in the building's security.

Sean had lost more than his group. He had lost everyone who he considered to be a friend, while some were more like family to him than his own flesh and blood. He wiped away tears of pain and rage as he looked at the building where his friends died. He wanted to get revenge, wanted to kill Conrad Burke, but doubted he would ever get the chance.

No, Burke was now out of reach, but there was someone else he could kill. It was a man who was being credited with bravery and hailed a hero. That man would be easier to kill, because he was in the hospital.

Sean clenched his hands into fists whenever he thought about Deke Mercer, a man he considered a traitor to his race. He had read about Deke's battle to survive; however, that morning's paper was full of good news about the man.

Apparently, Deke Mercer would live. He had successfully battled a lung infection. It was reported that he was expected to be moved out of intensive care and placed in a regular hospital room. There were even instructions in the article about how to leave flowers and gifts for the man.

Sean wiped at the last of his tears as a smile lit his face. The fools buying flowers should hold off on sending them to the hospital. In a day or two, they could send those flowers to a funeral home instead. Sean decided that he was going to kill Deke Mercer, and God help anyone who stood in his way.

Deputy Ralston dropped Tanner off in front of his house on Gentry Court, then backed up his police cruiser into the driveway of Tanner's neighbor, Josie Anderson.

Tanner already knew that Ralston and Josie were sleeping together, but he thought it bold for the cop to do so during the day, when Josie's husband could come home, and all the neighbors were out and about. When Ralston noticed Tanner looking at him, he pointed at the Anderson's home.

"Um, Mrs. Anderson has some clothes for a police charity drive. I figured I might as well pick them up while I'm in the area."

"I see," Tanner said, but he didn't care about Ralston's excuse for visiting his neighbor. Tanner wouldn't care if Ralston screwed Josie on the front lawn.

Back at the police station, Ralston's boss, Chief Ellison, was thinking about Tanner, the man he knew as Tom Myers. He chuckled as he remembered Jim Brett's futile efforts to land a punch on Myers, then he recalled that Myers had already had late night company in his home before they showed up. One of them was Josie Anderson, Tom Myers' neighbor, and a woman that the town grapevine had labeled a slut. The chief didn't care who slept with whom or how many, as long as it didn't lead to anything illegal.

At least one of the other women was a neighbor of Myers, and likely all of them were. They would mean they were also the wives of the neighborhood watch group. As Ellison recalled seeing them, he remembered that they were dressed in black.

It all came together for him in a flash, and Chief Ellison realized he had been looking at the wrong group of spouses. The vigilantes weren't those bozos from the neighborhood watch group, it was their damn wives.

The chief sat back in his chair, shook his head, and laughed. "I'll be damned."

Tanner entered his home to find that Alexa was in a good mood. She had read the news in the paper about Deke's recovery.

"He even sent me a text with the help of a nurse. He wants to see me tomorrow."

"Give him my thanks when you see him."

"You could come too, you know?"

"No, I can't, or don't you remember why you were going to the Burke campus in the first place?"

The smile left Alexa's face. "No, I remember. I was going to tell him that I never wanted to see him again."

"Which is a lie," Tanner said.

Alexa opened her mouth to deny it, but then nodded. "I like Deke, and yes, I would like him to stay in my life. How do you feel about that?"

Tanner took her in his arms. "I'll never ask you to deny yourself. You have feelings for the man, but you're with me. If you ever want more from Deke than friendship, let me know and I'll be on my way."

Alexa looked up into his face. "I don't think of him that way, really I don't. But Tanner, do you ever feel as if I'm asking you to deny yourself?"

"Yes."

"Because I want to live a normal life?"

"And I want to stay a Tanner."

Alexa's eyes began to tear up. "Why is it so hard to stay happy?"

Tanner chuckled. "It's the world of opposites that we live in. Black and white, up and down, in and out, happy and unhappy. It's inescapable."

Alexa wiped at her tears and kissed Tanner. "You recently asked me if I was happy. Are you happy?"

Tanner brushed back her long hair with his hand. "You've made me as happy as I've ever been, and no matter what happens in the future, nothing can take that away."

Alexa hugged him. "Just hold me for a while, okay?"

"Yes," Tanner said, and the two of them held each other while wondering where fate would take them.

7

GIFT GIVING, THE BILLIONAIRE WAY

TANNER ARRIVED AT THE LAKE AND SAW THAT THERE HAD been a few changes.

There was a huge blue and white RV, a recreational vehicle, set atop a space near the lake that had been cleared of trees to hold it. There was also a tank of natural gas for fuel. A twin of the mammoth vehicle sat on the other side of the lake. The second RV was green and white, and a new road diverged off the old one that wound around to it.

The old road had been gravel, but the old and new road were freshly paved. There was also a walking path that connected one RV to the other. The roads and the path had solar lighting along their edges to light them up at night. The shack still remained, and Tanner waited by it for Burke's arrival.

His wait was a short one, and Burke arrived in a limo with three security guards, and a woman that Tanner had never seen before. Sara followed behind them in her own vehicle.

One of the security guards had a keen eye. He asked

Tanner if the slight bulge in his pocket was a weapon. When Tanner said it was, all three men placed their hands on their guns while sheltering Burke behind them.

Burke told the men that Tanner was allowed to be armed in his presence and the guards relaxed, slightly.

The woman Tanner didn't know was Amanda Zwicky. She sent Tanner a shy smile as Sara introduced them.

"It's nice to meet you, Tanner. I understand you saved Mr. Burke's life."

"Burke was doing okay; he was just outgunned."

"Bullshit!" Burke said. "God knows where I'd be right now if not for you, and Miss Blake, I owe her for saving my wife."

"Why are we meeting here, Burke?" Tanner said. "Do you have work for me?"

"Ah, no Tanner, also, Miss Zwicky has yet to be brought up to speed on what it is you do."

"I see, so why the meeting?"

Burke grinned, then headed down a fresh section of road that led to the nearest RV.

"I'm here to thank you and Miss Blake. Please, both of you, follow me down to the lake. We'll walk, since it's such a beautiful day."

Everyone did as Burke said, but two of his security people moved forward to precede him. Tanner could tell that the men were well trained, and despite Burke's praise, they all kept an eye on him. They had marked him as a dangerous man and were being cautious.

After their party reached the first RV, Burke opened the lock on the door and invited everyone inside. The RV was new and beautiful, and bigger than many apartments.

"What is this, Burke, your new bachelor pad? Did your wife kick you out?"

"No Tanner, in fact, this RV belongs to you, as my gift."

"Miss Blake, you might have taken note that there is a duplicate RV on the other side of the lake. That one is yours."

Sara blinked in surprise. "Sir, thank you, that's incredibly generous. I know that these vehicles do not come cheap."

Burke grinned. "They're a pittance compared to your other gift."

"I have another gift?" Sara said.

"Yes, both you and Tanner, you see, Miss Blake, I no longer own this land, you and Tanner do. This side of the lake is Tanner's property, while the other side is yours. When I said that you two had my gratitude, I sure as hell meant it."

Tanner and Sara both stared at Burke as if they were waiting for the punch line. When he just kept grinning at them, they stared at each other.

Tanner held out his hand. "Hello, neighbor."

Sara took his hand and shook it, then began to giggle. She fell into one of the captain chairs in front of the dashboard and swiveled about in the cushioned seat.

"Are you really giving me half this land, Mr. Burke?"

"Yes, absolutely, of course, you'll have to accept it, as will Tanner."

Sara was still reeling from Burke's revelation.

"When you said you were going to build homes here someday, I planned to buy one. So yes, I'll take it. Thank you so much. It's truly beyond generous."

"You saved my wife. I can never repay that."

"I hope you're just as generous with Garber and Deke, Burke," Tanner said. "From what I hear, those two did as much as Sara and me. And Deke paid a steep price."

"Mr. Garber and his men have all received tokens of my appreciation. As a matter of fact, two of Garber's men retired early with the money I gave them. Mr. Mercer will never have to work again either, unless he wants to."

Burke reached into an inside pocket of his suit coat and removed an envelope, which he handed to Tanner.

"Please deliver that check to Miss Lucia for me. Mr. Garber told me that Alexa had been instrumental in taking back the cafeteria and freeing the hostages."

Tanner smiled and shook his hand. "You're all right, Burke, you really are, but what about Sloane Lennox, has he recovered yet?"

Burke laughed. "Sloan is taking a few weeks off at the advice of his doctor, but he'll be back."

"He did have a close call," Tanner said.

"One more thing," Burke said. "From this point on, you'll be briefed about new assignments at a different location. That decision came from Thomas Lawson. I understand that we'll be given more information soon."

"What is Lawson's story, Burke?"

"Your guess is as good as mine, Tanner, but the man has more political clout than I've ever seen. If he asks for something, he gets it. I assume it's because he produces results."

"And will I be working soon?"

"It's doubtful from what Lawson said, it seems that an assignment was in the works in Africa but was handled by someone else."

"Someone else?"

"A Mr. White, I believe you know him. Lawson said that the assignment was more suited to him than you, and I believe he didn't work alone."

"Hmm," Tanner said. "I'll have to ask White about that if I see him again."

"You expect to see Mr. White?" Burke asked.

"No, but I've a feeling our paths will cross again."

Zwicky cleared her throat, and everyone looked at her.

"When will I be brought up to speed on what it is that Tanner does for the company?"

Burke gestured at Sara. "Miss Blake, we'll drive around and let you have a look at your RV. While we're walking back to the limousine, why don't you fill Miss Zwicky in on what it is that Tanner does."

"Yes sir."

Sara left the RV with Zwicky trailing behind. Tanner followed everyone out, but then said that he would stay and explore his own RV. Zwicky shook his hand.

"It's been a pleasure to meet you, Tanner."

"Same here, Miss Zwicky."

"Oh, call me Amanda."

"I'll do that, and congratulations on your promotion."

AFTER LEAVING TANNER'S RV, ZWICKY GRIPPED SARA'S arm. "Oh my God, but that man is hot."

Sara smiled. "Tanner does have a way about him, yes."

"What does he do, and why is it so mysterious?"

INSIDE THE RV, TANNER WATCHED THE OTHERS WALK AWAY. Sara and Zwicky were in the lead, and Sara was telling Zwicky about his profession, and why he was at Burke.

He knew that Sara had gotten to the point when Zwicky suddenly stopped. She asked a question that Sara nodded yes to, then Zwicky looked back at his RV with her mouth hanging open slightly in shock.

Zwicky and Sara resumed walking, but every few steps, Zwicky would turn her head and stare back at his RV. Tanner wondered how Zwicky would react toward him at their next meeting. One thing was for certain, he'd made an impression.

He walked around the RV for a few minutes as he became familiar with the huge beast of a vehicle. Afterwards, he settled behind the steering wheel and called Alexa.

When she answered, he began by saying six words. "You're not going to believe this."

8

THE DEAL

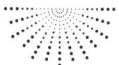

IN KILLBURRY, HODGES WAS GIVING A TOUR TO A MEMBER of the Brotherhood's council.

The man's name was Chang, and he had been a member of the Brotherhood since the days when it was solely comprised of Chinese. Chang was the guiding force behind the organization's expansion. What was once a gang of eight Chinese youths had grown to be an army of nearly a thousand men.

Chang stood just under six feet tall, wore his hair slicked back, and was well dressed in a gray suit. He was accompanied by several bodyguards, and Adán.

Hodges had his son, Dexter, at his side. The young man was dressed well in a black suit with a charcoal-hued shirt and red tie. Dexter had even gotten a haircut. Hodges thought his Uncle Mike was right, Dexter did resemble Hodge's late father a great deal.

Choa walked along between the two groups. He worked for Hodges but was Adán's cousin.

As the assemblage moved about, Hodges commented on the homes. Chang showed no reaction to anything he said, and Hodges wondered if that was good or bad. The homes were maintained as a matter of course, but Hodges had kept Pete and Rocco working hard. He'd made sure that the front of each property was swept clean and that the lawns had been cut.

The homes weren't new by any means. Few of them contained even a stick of furniture, but they were habitable. They would make good barracks for troops or could be used for storage.

Once the group was done looking about, the party returned to Hodges' house and sat in his office. Two of Chang's bodyguards stood outside the door, while two more flanked the chair he sat in. Hodges was seated with Dexter on an old leather sofa, and Adán and Choa stood in front of Hodges' desk, just taking it all in.

"So, Mr. Chang, what do you think? Do we have a deal?"

Chang spoke in a soft voice, but his English was excellent, although it carried a slight accent.

"Your houses, they're not bad, but we will need more from you if we're to come to an agreement."

Hodges face fell. He had hoped there wouldn't be any bullshit. "When you say, 'more', what do you mean by that?"

"There is no furniture. Do you expect the men to sleep on the floor?"

"No, but I thought that someone else could handle that."

"There is help available. As fate would have it, some of the members of the Brotherhood have an undertaking in the works. It involves pilfering the storage warehouse of a furniture manufacturer."

Hodges smiled. "All right then, problem solved. They can bring the goods right here once they have them."

"These men do not work for free and would expect compensation."

"From me?"

"Of course, as I said, we have no need for empty houses. You must furnish them first, and through these men, but you'll be given a very good price."

"How much are we talking about?"

Chang named a number and Hodges swallowed hard. It was an amount he had, but just barely. He would also need the money back that he had given his Uncle Mike to hold.

"Okay, let's say that I agree, then do we have a deal? You get the houses… furnished houses, and I get a seat on the Brotherhood Council, yes?"

"No," Chang said.

"No? Why not?"

"We would require one more thing from you."

"Yeah?"

"The houses, this house included, would all have to be signed over to a corporation that is owned by the Brotherhood."

Hodges just sat with his mouth open, stunned by Chang's gall. He was asking him to sign over his life. Once he did so, why would they need him? Hodges might have been too stunned to speak, but Dexter found his voice.

"Yo, dude, do you think my father is an idiot? There's no way we're signing that deal."

"Be quiet, boy," Chang said. "Men are speaking."

"Fuck you! I'm a man."

Both of Chang's bodyguards took out their weapons and pointed them at Dexter. Chang softly said, "No," and the guns went back inside their holsters.

"What the hell?" Hodges said. "My kid didn't even show a weapon."

"You should teach your boy about respect," Chang said, "or others will do so."

Hodges glared at Dexter, but when he looked back at Chang, he shook his head.

"My son needs to learn when to talk and when not to talk, I agree, but I don't disagree with what he said. I'll give the Brotherhood the use of the houses, and I'll even pony up the cash for the furniture, but Chang, the houses stay mine."

"Is that your final word, Mr. Hodges?"

"It's gonna have to be, yeah, and I think it's a good deal for both of us."

Chang stood. "I will relay your offer to the rest of the Brotherhood Council, and we will give you an answer soon."

Hodges stood as well, along with Dexter. "Good, and thanks for coming."

Chang sent Hodges a nod, and then stared at Dexter until the young man looked away. Chang left town without delay, but Adán said he was going to stay around and catch up with Choa.

"Great," Hodges said. "And Choa, take the rest of the day off. If there's a problem, I'll handle it."

"Thanks boss," Choa said.

After everyone left, Hodges slapped Dexter lightly on the cheek and smiled.

"You say, 'Fuck you' to a man like Chang? You've got stones, Dexter."

Dexter grinned. "Thanks Dad, but his deal is bullshit."

"It's just business hardball, but it's a good deal and the Brotherhood will take it. Once they do, we have it made. As a member of the Brotherhood Council, I'll be raking in a percentage of everything the Brotherhood takes in. We'll also make money off their men."

"How do we make money off the men?"

"Think about it, son. Once the men are here, we'll run some poker games, sell them drugs, booze… and women. The two of us will make money coming and going."

"Dad."

"Yeah?"

"Let me handle the women."

Hodges laughed. "Tony will handle the women, that's his job, but I guess he might need some help."

Dexter was smiling, but then grew serious. "Is this really going to happen?"

"Yeah, Dexter, I think the Hodges are getting back on top in Killburry. But listen, I need you to do me a favor."

"What's that?"

"Go to Hartford and see your Uncle Mike. Do you remember him?"

"A little, but I haven't seen him in years."

"I'll call ahead and tell him that you're coming. He'll give you a package that I need."

Dexter looked down at himself. "I like wearing a suit."

Hodges smiled at his son. "Most men do."

9

BLOOD TRUMPS EVERYTHING

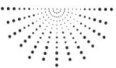

Burke had told Sara to follow along behind the limo in her own car when they were headed to the lake property. She realized why, as she examined her new RV. Burke had known that she would want to stay behind and explore her new toy.

When a knock came at the door, it startled her. Since they were the only ones on the property, Sara assumed it was Tanner, but she called out anyway.

"Who's there?"

"Who do you think it is, Bigfoot?"

After inviting him in, they sat together in her kitchen nook.

"Do you believe this?" Sara asked as she looked around.

"I do, but it's a hell of a surprise."

"I've never driven one of these, have you?"

"Yes, and the last time was in Las Vegas, it was on the day we met."

Sara's eyes widened as she remembered the RV that Tanner had rigged to blow up at Al Rossetti's desert home.

She gave him a playful punch on the arm. "I remember now, and a flaming chunk of that damn thing nearly hit me."

Tanner rubbed his arm as if she'd hurt him. "It wasn't intentional."

They grinned at each other as they locked eyes. The silence seemed to last too long, and Sara broke it with a question.

"So, neighbor, why did you stop by?"

"I'm here to issue you an invitation. Alexa wants you to come for dinner tomorrow in Killburry. Can you make it?"

Sara smiled. "Yes, and thanks, I'm curious to see where you live."

"It's just a house, Blake, I mean, Sara. It's nothing too fancy."

"Still, it's the thought of you living in a neighborhood, cutting the grass, waving to a passerby as you stoop to pick up the morning paper. It's too normal for you, Tanner."

"It's not as normal as you might think, and neither are my neighbors."

"What's so odd about your neighbors?"

Tanner went on to tell Sara about his night, about Bart McGurn, and also about being summoned to the police station. When he was done, Sara was laughing.

"I should have known that nothing about you would be normal. You move into an area with a low crime rate and live next door to the town's most wanted."

"Oh, there are a few real tough guys. The main one is named Burt Hodges. His son is a punk, and the two of us had a run-in."

Sara looked around. "Damn, I wish I had some coffee to go with these stories."

"There's some back at the shack."

"Really? Okay, let's go there. But since when is there a coffeemaker at the shack?"

"I've been fixing the place up. It's livable now, and Burke even had the town run a power line in. Of course, who needs it with the RV's?"

They had stepped outside and were walking to Sara's car. She turned, looked at the RV, and sighed. "I still have trouble believing that belongs to me. If Mr. Burke had been more patient, he might have built us homes."

As they drove to the shack, Tanner began telling Sara about his run-in with Dexter, and Hodges' late-night visit to his house to save his son.

"But your neighbors had already knocked the boy out?"

"They had him bound and ready to ship back home when his father showed up."

"Hodges sounds like trouble."

"Nothing I can't handle."

Once they were at the shack, Sara made coffee and they sat outside at the picnic table. When Sara brought up the subject of Deke, Tanner told her that Alexa planned to visit Deke the next day.

"That's good. She'll lift his spirits."

"I'm just glad that he's healing. I owe him too. He saved Alexa before you did."

"Why were you two headed to Burke that day?"

"Alexa was going there to tell Deke goodbye."

Sara looked surprised. "Was something going on between them?"

"No, but Deke wants her."

"And now?"

"And now they'll remain friends."

"His feelings won't change. I actually think he might love her, at least a little."

"A little?" Tanner said. "Is love something that can be done in half measures?"

"No, but it can creep up on you... or so I've been told."

"It sounds like a staph infection," Tanner said, and Sara laughed.

AT THE HOSPITAL, THE SOLE SURVIVING NEO-NAZI, SEAN, was sitting in the lobby. He was pretending to read a newspaper as he listened to the conversations around him.

When an elderly black couple asked for a visitor's pass for their grandson, Sean heard the man clearly enunciate the grandson's name. Then, the man and his wife discussed how horrible it was that the young man had been injured in an accident at work, which apparently was a fall.

Once the couple left the desk and entered an elevator, Sean stood and walked outside, where he sat on a bench and waited.

The elderly couple left the hospital about an hour later. Sean gave it another ten minutes, and then he walked inside and asked for a visitor's pass by using the name of the couple's grandson.

The pass was granted, and Sean walked by the security guard while barely receiving a look.

He found the grandson on the sixth floor. The man was in his early twenties. His head was bandaged and there was a cast on his right leg. He also had two IV's attached to an arm. Sean surmised that the man would still be there tomorrow and that there was no fear of him being discharged.

That was good, that meant that he could enter the hospital the next day, use the man's name to acquire a visitor's pass, and then be free to roam the halls. He had been standing in the doorway and staring in at the elderly couple's grandson while thinking, and the man had taken note.

"Hey guy, can I help you?"

"You already have, Midnight."

"Midnight? What the hell do you mean by that?"

Sean ignored him, returned to the visitor's desk and handed in his pass. He had plans to return the next day, find Deke Mercer, and kill him.

Sean smiled as he fingered the knife in his pocket. People die in the hospital all the time.

BACK IN KILLBURRY, CHOA WAS BEING ASKED BY HIS Cousin Adán to make a decision. He was at his house in Killburry, his free house, which Hodges had given him to live in. Choa and Adán were sitting in the living room. There was a baseball game on, but the sound had been turned down while the two men discussed business.

Choa shook his head and sighed. "Does it really have to go down that way, Adán?"

"Hodges is in the way. Chang gave him the chance to give us what we want, but he said no."

"He didn't say no; he just doesn't want to be pushed out. If he signs over everything, then he knows he won't be needed."

"He's not needed, Choa. Don't you see that? He was a fool to come to us when he's got no way to protect himself. Chang wasn't lying. He will take Hodges' offer to the council, but they're hard men, practical men, and they'll just take what they want."

"So, he's fucked either way?"

"Yeah, man, he was fucked the second he called me. He should have just kept his head down and stayed out of the way, but no, he wants to be a player. He ain't no player."

"What do you want me to do, kill him?"

"No, Chang's people will handle that, but you will have to prove your loyalty to join the Brotherhood. The thing is, Hodges told me that he's got someone who will go to Pullo in New York and the Irish mob in Boston if anything happens to him. I need to know who that is. We have to take care of that man before we make our move. If Joe Pullo learned what we were planning, we'd lose the element of surprise, you know?"

"Yeah, so you want me to rat on my friends?"

"No, I want you to show loyalty to me, your cousin, your blood. I'll look out for you, Choa, you know that. You can join my crew and make twice the cash Hodges is paying you. Tell me, do you know who Hodges picked to warn Pullo?"

Choa said nothing, and Adán got a worried look on his face.

"Oh shit, please tell me that it's not you."

"No, it ain't me, but yeah, I know who it is. It's a black dude named Tony, a pimp. He runs a few girls for Hodges."

Adán took out his phone. "Where can this Tony be found?"

Choa hesitated again. He and Tony were friends, and he even liked his boss, Hodges. Then he looked at Adán, and he remembered all the times they saved each other's asses as they were growing up. Blood trumps everything.

"I know where to find Tony," Choa said, and so began his betrayal of Burt Hodges.

10

IT'S JUST BUSINESS

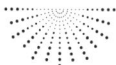

DEXTER SPUN HIS COUSIN ANNA AROUND IN THE AIR BY holding her under her arms and then sat the giggling girl back on the ground. His broken wrist ached some from the effort, but Dexter liked making his little cousin happy. When he offered the same ride to his other cousin, Jack, the boy shook his head.

"I'm too old to be spun around like a kid."

Dexter tousled the boy's hair. "Don't be in a hurry to grow up; it's not as cool as it looks."

As his father requested, Dexter had gone to see his Uncle Mike. He had stayed for dinner, at his Cousin Sheila's insistence, and had the best meal he'd eaten since his mother had passed away years earlier.

As the kids moved inside to go to their rooms, Uncle Mike and Dexter settled on the front porch. Mike had already handed back the money that Hodges had given him to hold, but he wanted to ask Dexter about Killburry.

"Your dad told me about this Brotherhood thing, what do you think of it?"

Dexter shrugged. "They got juice and Dad wants to get plugged in. I think it will be good if they take the deal."

"What exactly is the deal?" Mike asked.

Dexter explained about his father's offer to trade the houses for a place on the Brotherhood's council. The more he talked, the more concerned Mike became.

"They won't make that deal. They'll just take what they want."

"How are they gonna do that?"

"I can think of a way, and your father wouldn't like it one bit."

"No, Uncle Mike, Dad knows what he's doing, you'll see."

Mike stared at his nephew, a boy who looked so much like his late brother.

"Dexter, listen to me. If things go sideways, you get the hell out of Killburry and come straight here. You can always come here, boy, you know?"

"Thanks, Uncle Mike; I'll remember that."

Mike pointed to the cast on Dexter's wrist. "Your father told me that a man named Myers gave you that. Have you had any more run-ins with him?"

"Nah, but Dad says we'll settle up with Tom Myers once we have the Brotherhood behind us."

Mike was lighting a cigar, and he spoke around it as the flame ignited the tobacco. "Where does this Myers live?"

"He's on the other side of that new park they built, on a dead-end street, but why do you want to know?"

Mike smiled, as he tried his best to look like a harmless old man. It was easier than he would have liked to admit.

"No reason, you just get curious when you're my age, that's all."

Dexter and Mike talked a little longer, and then Dexter went back to Killburry.

Uncle Mike also planned to visit Killbury. He was going to pay a visit to Tom Myers.

∼

Tony Washington was sitting in his car and listening to a jazz station out of New York City that he liked. He had dropped a girl off at a house in Farmington that was near a lake and was waiting for her to come out. It was a peaceful night and the station was playing a tribute to Miles Davis, whose music Tony loved.

He was feeling all mellow when the front door of the house flew open and the girl came running out and toward the car. She had only been inside for a short time, and from the look on her face, Tony knew there was trouble.

He stepped out of the car just as the girl reached it. The girl's name was Trina. Trina was a natural blonde with hair down to her ass. Tony took her by the shoulders and asked her what was wrong.

"The guy paid, we fucked, and then the asshole took my purse and wouldn't give it back," Trina said.

Tony cursed. Normally, he would call Choa to come and handle the problem, but Hodges had given Choa the night off. That meant that either Tony handled it himself or he had to call Hodges.

Tony was still considering things when the man came out of the house carrying Trina's purse. He was a white guy, no bigger than Tony, and so Tony figured he'd handle it.

The man walked over, ignored him, and grabbed Trina by the arm. "C'mon, sweet thing, we need to talk. For one thing, I'm your new boss."

Tony laughed as he took out his gun. "What the fuck

are you smokin'? Now let the bitch go and give her back her purse before I shoot your crazy ass."

The man sent Tony a smile, then he looked over Tony's shoulder. "You got this, right?"

Tony was turning his head to see who the man was speaking to and felt a fist slam into his right temple. Tony tumbled to the ground, dropping the gun as he fell. By the time he regained his senses, he realized he was back behind the wheel of his car.

"What the hell…?" he mumbled.

"I'm sorry, dude. It's just business," said a familiar voice from the passenger seat.

Tony turned his head and saw Choa. "What the fuck, man? Did you hit me?"

"Goodbye, Tony," Choa said. He placed the gun against the very spot he had landed the earlier punch and shot Tony in the head. Blood splattered the windshield as the side window shattered.

Choa had used Tony's own gun to kill him. Choa wiped the weapon off, made sure that Tony's prints would be found on it, and dropped the gun onto the floor between Tony's feet.

On the radio, Miles Davis' Seven Steps to Heaven was playing.

Choa headed back to Killburry. He was now a member of the Brotherhood.

Anna, Louise, Tina, and Josie waved to their husbands from Tanner's porch, as the men made their rounds while patrolling the neighborhood. Their children were being babysat, but Anna had her daughter with her.

The child was asleep in her arms, after having just consumed a bottle of formula.

Tanner and Alexa were acting as hosts, and had brought out cheese, crackers, and wine.

Alexa pointed at the ladies' husbands. "Have they ever caught a burglar?"

The women all laughed. "If that ever happened, we'd have to buy them capes," Anna said.

After realizing that no one had seen Bart or June McGurn all day, Josie told everyone that she had her husband, Ted, check out the McGurn's home. Ted was a real estate agent, and he discovered that the home was owned by Silicon City.

Louise nodded knowingly. "That's not too surprising. In the past, Silicon City would use the house for executives and their families. It was for people who were moving here but had yet to buy a home or were waiting a day or two for their furniture to arrive. I just assumed that the McGurns had bought the house from Silicon City."

"Why would Silicon City care about trapping a group of vigilantes?" Tina asked.

"Face it, that corporation owns Killburry," Anna said. "I guess they want to protect the town's image as a low crime paradise."

Tanner told the ladies about his meeting with Chief Ellison, and they said that they would cool things for a while. When he mentioned the chief's daughter, Olivia, Tanner learned something about the young lady.

"She can shoot?" Tanner said.

"We go to the same shooting range," Anna said. "That girl is awesome with a rifle, and she's got the eye of an eagle."

"I'll keep that in mind."

Josie smiled at Tanner. "She's also very cute, did you notice?"

"All I saw was a uniform and a badge," Tanner said, and Alexa laughed.

"Liar, I saw you looking her over when she came to the door."

"Looking," Tanner said, "just looking."

The ladies stayed a little longer, but when the baby woke, they called it a night.

Josie sent Tanner a little wave. "Nighty-night, Tom, and if for any reason you can't sleep, you can always just give me a ring and we'll—"

"Careful," Alexa said, as she grabbed the knife she had used to slice the cheese.

Josie departed without saying another word.

"I think she was impressed by the way you handled that knife last night," Tanner said.

"She's still a flirt, but I did notice that she sat as far away from you as she could get."

Alexa gathered up the cheese, crackers, and wine glasses, but Tanner told her to leave his glass, the bottle, and another glass that hadn't been used.

"Why, are you expecting another guest?"

"He's already here," Tanner said.

Alexa had to force herself not to look around. "Who is it?"

"An old man. He's been watching us from the woods for about ten minutes."

"What do you want to do?"

"You go inside, and I'll see what he wants."

"All right, but why can't we just have a normal night?"

"I'm sure it's nothing, but stay alert until I come in."

Alexa carried the tray inside. When the old man didn't

move, Tanner raised up his wine glass and called to him. "It's good wine, why don't you join me?"

A few moments passed, and then the old man walked out of the woods and over to Tanner's house. It was Hodges' Uncle Mike.

He sent Tanner a nod, poured a glass of wine, and took the seat at Tanner's left. "How did you spot me?"

"Your watch, it reflected the streetlights when you moved."

Mike looked down at his wrist in disgust. In the old days, he never would have forgotten to remove it.

"You're Tom Myers, right?"

"Yeah."

"Well Myers, it sucks getting old."

Tanner raised his glass. "It's still better than the alternative."

Mike laughed, then raised his glass as well. "You're right there."

They sat together for a moment in silence, then, Mike spoke.

"My name is Mike Hodges, I came here to see the man who broke my nephew's wrist."

"Did your nephew tell you that he pulled a knife on me, after stealing an old lady's purse?"

"No, he didn't, but he's still my nephew."

"I hear you," Tanner said.

Silence returned, and this time it was Tanner who broke it.

"What was this about, Mike, vengeance? Are you here to get payback?"

"The thought crossed my mind, but I think I just wanted to see you. My other nephew, Burt, he said that you were with the Giacconi Family and in tight with Joe Pullo."

"I'm not with the Giacconi Family, but I do know Pullo well. Do you know him too?"

"I met Pullo a long time ago when he was just coming up. He impressed me then. But tell me, why does he care about this town?"

"He doesn't, this is just where I happened to buy a house. If Burt Hodges is worried about me moving in on his turf, you can tell him to relax."

"I'll do that the next time I see him."

They sat in silence again, then watched as the neighborhood patrol walked around the cul-de-sac in their bright yellow shirts and blindingly white caps. Since it was a warm night, they were all wearing white shorts that matched the caps. As the men started back the way they came, Mike pointed at them.

"What the fuck was that, the world's smallest gay pride parade?"

Tanner grinned. "Those are the brave men of our neighborhood watch group."

"Good God."

"Yeah."

Mike stood. "Thanks for the wine, Myers, and the talk."

"You're welcome. Stop by sometime but skip the standing in the woods part."

"I might do that, Myers. And hey, is there a shortcut back to the park? That's where I left my car."

"Cut through my yard; there's a gate there."

"Good, that damn walk through the woods winded me. It sucks getting old, and let me tell you, it comes quicker than you think."

"Goodnight, Mike."

"Yeah, yeah," Mike said, as he disappeared around the back of the house.

11
THE ANSWER

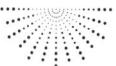

Alexa stepped onto the porch. "What was that about with the old man?"

"That was another Hodges, Mike Hodges, and he's all right."

"Can't we have just one night when nothing happens?"

"I didn't invite him, Alexa."

"I know. I just want things to be peaceful here. Is that too much to ask?"

Tanner stood and grabbed up the wine and the glasses.

"Let's go inside. I've seen enough of the neighborhood watch."

They went into the kitchen and Alexa asked Tanner if he had invited Sara over to the house.

"She'll be here tomorrow, but we're going out to eat, right?"

"Yes, I would cook, but I want to see Deke and I'm not sure what time I'll get back from the hospital. He's also having some tests done, so I won't be able to visit him early."

"He's out of intensive care?"

Alexa pointed to the white board that was on the wall by the phone. "That's his room number along with his phone number. He called earlier but couldn't speak for long. He's still quite weak."

Tanner nodded. "I remember what it's like to be that weak after a shooting. There were days I wondered if I'd ever heal."

"And you were alone too," Alexa said. "That must have been horrible."

"It was horrible, but I wasn't alone, I had Spenser."

They cleaned the glasses, checked the locks, and set the alarm. Alexa had showered first, and when Tanner came out of the bathroom, he climbed into bed beside her. Alexa stirred, but didn't wake.

Tanner laid there for nearly two hours before falling asleep. He kept feeling as if something were wrong, and his eyes would spring open whenever he closed them. After checking the house, along with the deck and the porch, Tanner reset the alarm and went back to bed.

His sense of danger was keen, but he wasn't the one in peril.

ON THE OTHER SIDE OF THE PARK, AT THE HOME OF BURT Hodges, several men were silently entering Hodges' home through the back door. Two of the men carried sheets of clear plastic along with an assortment of instruments, including a hacksaw and a blowtorch. Those two men went down into the basement, while four of the other men continued up the stairs. Two of those men entered Dexter's bedroom, while the other two went for Hodges.

Hodges awoke, but he was too groggy from sleep to resist the hands that gripped him. He was soon lying on his stomach with his wrists and ankles bound and a ball gag in his mouth.

When Dexter cried out from the other room, Hodges went mad trying to free himself, but only managed to become sweaty and exhausted. Minutes passed, and the men around him just leaned back against the walls as if they were waiting for something.

When Hodges noticed that they were all Asians, he thought of Chang, and knew that the men had something to do with the Brotherhood. None of his captors said a word until one of them received a call.

The man removed the phone from his pocket, listened, then uttered a few words in Cantonese. After putting his phone away, he said something to the other men, and they all donned gloves. Next, Hodges was lifted off the bed and carried downstairs while facing upward. The sensation of traveling that way made him feel odd, but he was far too scared to be affected much by the peculiar angle and motion.

Once they were on the bottom floor, the men carried him through a hallway and then down into the basement. All of Hodges' things had been pushed aside to make room in a corner. Clear, thick plastic hung down from the ceiling to form a wall. The space beyond could be entered by pushing through a slit in the plastic, which had been sliced down its middle.

As he was carried inside, Hodges saw that the entire area was covered in plastic.

Dexter was sitting in a chair with his ankles and wrists duct taped to the chair's arms and legs. He also had a ball gag in his mouth, while his eyes were wide with terror.

"Mr. Hodges, look at me, Mr. Hodges."

It was Chang. He was wearing a raincoat, the slick yellow kind like kids wore. He also wore matching boots and a pair of black leather gloves. In his right hand was a hacksaw.

When Chang saw that he had Hodges' attention, he spoke again.

"As I said earlier, I would talk to the other council members and return to give you their reply. This is our answer. We reject your offer, and you will sign over the houses to us."

Chang nodded toward a man who was dressed in a clear plastic raincoat and pants. Hodges could tell that the man wore a suit beneath the plastic. He was also the only non-Asian.

"That man is a former member of the criminal organization known as the Conglomerate. He is now a member of the Brotherhood and is very skilled in legal matters. You will sign the documents that he has prepared. And yes, I know that you do not want to. That is why I will start by giving you incentive to cooperate."

Chang said something in Cantonese and those who weren't wearing rain suits donned them. Once they were all covered up to their necks, they added clear face masks and hats. With everyone ready, Chang gripped Dexter by the hair, yanked his head back, and smiled.

"Earlier, you spoke to me with disrespect. Now, I will teach you manners."

Chang released Dexter, even as another of the men held Dexter's right arm firmly to the chair. An instant later, Chang was ripping through Dexter's arm with the hacksaw, at a point that was right above the cast on his wrist, spewing blood everywhere.

Behind their ball gags, the Hodges screamed, one from physical pain, the other from the anguish of failing his son so horribly. By the time the sun rose on a new day, the Brotherhood owned Hodges' properties.

Chang claimed Hodges house for himself and made it the headquarters of the Brotherhood's new home. Down in the basement, not a trace of blood could be found.

Burt and Dexter Hodges were also nowhere in sight, and their bodies would never be discovered.

12

A BAD FEELING

The following morning, Alexa kissed Tanner goodbye before climbing into her car. She was leaving to pay Deke a visit in the hospital but planned to be back in time to take Sara to dinner.

Alexa rolled down her car window. "Stay away from Josie while I'm gone, and that cute cop too."

Tanner cocked an eyebrow at her. "I'm not the one going off to visit their boyfriend."

"Stop that. Deke is just a friend and you know it."

"I was kidding. Tell Deke that we'll have him here for a visit once he's better."

"Really?"

"Yes, like I said, I owe him for saving you, and I'm not the jealous type. Besides, if he ever touched you, I'd just kill him."

"But you're not the jealous type?"

"Not at all."

They kissed again, and before she drove off, Alexa had a request.

"Please don't get into any trouble."

"I don't plan to. I have some language study to do and then I'm going to watch a ballgame until Sara arrives."

Alexa smiled. "That sounds harmless."

A few seconds later, Alexa was gone. Tanner found that he missed her immediately, while the house behind him seemed like a big empty box.

He sighed. "Maybe we should get a dog."

On the other side of the park, things were moving fast as Chang prepared for the first meeting of the Brotherhood Council in their new home. The furniture in Hodges' dining room had been removed and a conference table was set in its place.

Pete and Rocco were being used as free labor to get everything ready. The two teens had been forced into servitude and were bringing in the chairs for the conference table. The men who were given the task of making the boys work were a couple of gangbangers who had just been released from prison and hoped to join the Brotherhood officially.

One of them, a punk with a shaved head, named Reo, liked to pick on Rocco and called him retard. When Rocco pointed out to Reo that he wasn't being nice, Reo had beaten the young man. Pete attempted to stop it, and he took a beating from the other gangbanger, Dominic.

Choa entered the house. When he saw the swelling and bruises on Pete and Rocco's faces, he asked what happened.

"Retard here gave me and my boy some shit, so we fucked him and his brother up a little. They've been quiet ever since."

Choa scowled. He knew that Pete and Rocco were harmless, but it wasn't his problem, and so he moved toward the office to find Adán. Choa actually found his cousin in the kitchen, where Adán and his men were devouring two pizzas.

Adán smiled. "Choa, grab a slice and a beer, then follow me."

A minute later, Adán and Choa were sitting on Hodges' back porch and looking out at the small stream that ran behind it.

"There's a lot goin' on today, Choa, are you ready for some action?"

"Hell yeah, but what's up?"

"Today we wipe out the vigilantes, along with the police chief and his top men. We'll make it look like they all went after each other."

"How the hell do you do that?"

Adán pointed back at the kitchen. "You, me, and my guys will do a mass home invasion over on that dead-end street where the vigilantes live. This won't be a robbery. We do a lot of damage, kill a few people, and then leave behind some clues that point to the police. But before that happens, the chief of police will be put down, and we'll make it look like one of the vigilantes did it."

Choa looked confused. "Why would people think that cops did the home invasions?"

"Easy, we're only going to hit the homes of the people Chief Ellison suspects are the vigilantes. We'll be leaving shit behind that will have some of the cops' prints on it, and we'll also be using that special ammo the pigs use."

"Where did you get the cops' stuff?"

Adán leaned back in his seat. "Remember you told me about that dirty cop, Tim Ralston? We own his ass now. Chang is using him to kill the chief, but Ralston will be leaving behind evidence that one of the vigilantes' killed him. He's also the one who gave us the stuff from the police."

"Tim Ralston is going to kill the chief? How much are you paying him for that?"

"Nothing up front, but Chang told Ralston that he'll see that he's the new chief. The Brotherhood will rig the next election. In a town like this, that's easy."

"There's one thing you didn't think of, what about Tom Myers? I've met him, and he ain't no punk."

"I didn't forget him, he'll be ours. While some of the boys are handling things, we'll take four men with us and make sure he never tells Pullo shit about what we're doing here. The cops will be blamed for his death too."

"When is all this going down?"

"First the chief gets hit, and then we move on the vigilantes."

"Who is being framed for whacking the chief?"

"Ralston has been banging one of the vigilante's wives. He stole some stuff from her house yesterday when she was in the shower. He's going to leave behind a pen with the guy's prints on it. The man is a real estate agent, and we made it so he won't have an alibi. The woman he'll be showing a house to is one of our hookers using a fake ID. She'll disappear, and everyone will think he lied about showing a house."

"And the cops you're framing?"

"Ralston's handled that, he made sure they all had the day off. They're all fishing buddies. They'll be out on a boat, and fish can't offer alibis."

"It's slick, if everything goes just right, but Adán, don't underestimate this dude Tom Myers; I'm telling you, he's not a joke."

"Choa, there will be six of us going after his ass, he don't stand a chance."

"Yeah, I guess you're right," Choa said, but he still had a bad feeling.

13
MAN AND DOG

The neo-Nazi, Sean, was feeling frustrated as he walked the halls of the hospital. His plan to obtain a visitor's pass was a good one, but he had no idea what room Deke Mercer was in.

The hospital was twelve stories high and had hundreds of rooms. Still, he assumed that a man who had just been released from ICU would likely be placed in a room near the nurses' station. Also, given Deke's notoriety, his room should be bursting with flowers and cards full of get well wishes. Sean started looking into the rooms near the nurses' station on the first floor he checked, and then moved outward along the corridors from there.

When he stepped off the elevator to search a new floor, he saw the chart on the wall. The chart explained that some floors were zoned primarily for certain afflictions, while other floors serviced specific conditions.

Sean smiled. That eliminated several floors, such as the floors containing the children's ward and the one designated maternity. Sean then saw that the seventh floor was zoned for thoracic medicine and knew that had something to do with the torso. Deke Mercer had been wounded in the torso, so Sean was off to the seventh floor. As he stepped back onto the elevator, he played with the knife in his pocket.

∽

W̲h̲i̲l̲e̲ S̲e̲a̲n̲ w̲a̲s̲ g̲e̲t̲t̲i̲n̲g̲ o̲n̲ a̲n̲ e̲l̲e̲v̲a̲t̲o̲r̲ h̲e̲a̲d̲e̲d̲ f̲o̲r̲ the seventh floor, Alexa was stepping off of one on that very floor.

She was carrying a present for Deke, a cactus she had bought in the hospital gift shop. Although the plant was thorny, it was beautiful and would require little care. Alexa followed the signs to Deke's room number and saw that it was near the nurses' station. Alexa thought that was good, if Deke needed anything, his nurse would be nearby.

Deke was sitting up in bed but was asleep when she entered, and Alexa had a chance to observe him without being noticed. She had to fight back tears when she saw how small he looked. His injury, combined with the surgery, and his battle with infection had left Deke looking shrunken.

As Sean had surmised it would be, Deke's room was full of flowers and get well wishes, many of them were sent by the people who had been in the cafeteria with Deke when the attack occurred.

As Alexa set the plant on the table beside his bed, Deke's eyes opened. When he saw who had come to visit him, a wide smile appeared, and he spoke to her in a weak voice.

"Hello, pretty lady."

Alexa leaned over and kissed him on the cheek. "How do you feel, Deke?"

"I feel better now that I'm seeing you, and I'll heal."

Deke's voice was raspy, and Alexa grabbed a cup that had a built-in straw. After he took a few sips of water, Alexa was pleased to see that Deke's voice sounded stronger. He spoke to her again when he pointed at the cactus.

"Thank you for the gift. I like cactus."

Alexa looked at the plant and frowned when she noticed that there was dust on the pot the plant was in. She then looked down at her hands and saw that some of the dirt had transferred there.

"I have to wash my hands, but then I'll sit and visit with you."

"You've made my day by coming here, Alexa."

Alexa sent Deke a smile and then walked into the adjacent bathroom, but she left the door open since she only needed to wash her hands. She had taken the plant into the room with her, so that she could remove the rest of the dust from its ceramic pot.

She cleaned her hands, dampened some toilet paper, and began cleaning the pot. When she heard someone enter the room, Alexa assumed that it was a nurse, or perhaps another visitor.

Except Alexa felt a sudden sense of uneasiness. When Deke asked a question, it was answered, and Alexa was immediately on alert.

"Who are you?"

"Who am I? I'm the man whose friends you helped to kill at Burke Headquarters, and I'm here for payback."

Alexa peeked around the bathroom door and saw a man in his thirties with short brown hair. An instant later, a knife appeared in the man's right hand.

Alexa, who only wanted to live a life of peace going forward, was unarmed. She looked about the bathroom, searching desperately for something to use as a weapon.

She saw nothing, but knew she had to act before it was too late.

She moved silently toward Sean, but then saw him stiffen in alarm. It was the window; he had seen her reflection.

As Sean turned to face her with his knife, Alexa rushed forward, forced by fate back into violence.

Chief of Police John Ellison had a home on the river. It was one of several houses that sat on Killburry's western border.

It wasn't a huge house, but it had a little land around it, and he lived there with his daughter, Olivia. There was another family member as well, and that was the chief's dog, Seth. Seth was a German shepherd and a retired police dog from another town.

The chief was friends with Seth's human partner, and when it came time for the dog to retire, the chief took Seth in. He was an old dog that needed medication for a heart ailment, but Seth was still alert and very loving.

The chief was walking the dog on a leash, down by the river, which was only about fifty yards from his back door. He was looking down at Seth when he saw his hackles rise, then the hound's eyes looked along the riverbank, at the figure walking toward them.

Seth began barking furiously and the chief reined him in and studied the figure. It was a man wearing a bright yellow shirt with a white cap pulled down low over his eyes. The chief realized that the shirt and the hat looked familiar and remembered seeing the neighborhood watch group being dressed that way. When he saw that the man was holding one hand out of sight, Ellison went on full alert.

He was about to put his hand on his weapon when he recognized the man walking toward him and calmed down. Talking loudly to be heard over the dog's barking, Chief Ellison asked his visitor a question.

"Tim, why are you dressed like that?"

Deputy Tim Ralston answered his boss by revealing the gun he had hidden behind his back, which he then pointed at the chief's chest.

Thinking better of the situation, Ralston switched his aim to the dog. It would do him no good to kill the chief and have his throat ripped out by the dog's fangs. Ralston aimed directly at Seth's face and pulled the trigger. Seconds later, both man and dog lay on the ground, as the water lapped peacefully at the river's edge.

14
A THORNY SITUATION

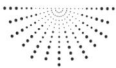

Alexa thrust the cactus at Sean's eyes as the neo-Nazi spun around with his blade.

The knife cut her left arm before Sean dropped it to reach for his eyes, which had been punctured or scratched by several needles.

Sean's screams of pain brought nurses, orderlies, and a doctor running into the room. They were soon joined by a security guard, and he was the one who spotted the swastika tattoo on the inside portion of Sean's wrist.

As Sean was being carted away, Alexa was escorted to a treatment room, where she would also be questioned when the police arrived.

Deke called to her. "Please come back before you leave. And thank you."

Alexa only had time to send him a smile before she was rushed out the door with her wounded arm dripping blood along the hallway.

Chief Ellison had inhaled sharply when he saw the gun in Ralston's hand. When Ralston lowered his aim to shoot the dog, the chief let go of the leash just as Ralston fired.

The shot was loud, and was followed by an echo, but the echo originated from the rear of the chief's house. Olivia stood with a rifle at her shoulder. She had shot Tim Ralston, just as Ralston was firing his own weapon.

The chief watched, as a bright red stain blossomed across Ralston's yellow shirt and astonishment bloomed on Ralston's face. Then, the deputy fell backwards, to lie motionless.

After kicking Ralston's gun away, the chief checked on his victim. The dog was down as well and had been shot in a rear leg. When the chief saw that the wound wasn't much more than a bad scratch, he prompted Seth to stand, and the hound made it to his feet and licked the chief's face.

Olivia came on the run, still holding her rifle, then skidded to a stop and stared down at Ralston.

"Oh my God. He's dead, isn't he?"

Ellison went to his daughter and held her. "You saved my life, baby."

"The dog, Seth, I heard him barking and saw a man walking toward you. From where I was, I could see the gun behind his back. I grabbed my rifle and… I shot him."

A sound came from Ralston's body. When the chief investigated, he found Ralston's phone. There was a new text. IS THE DEED DONE?

The chief and his daughter read it together.

"Oh my God, Dad. Tim was working with someone."

"Yeah, but who?" Ellison said, then he keyed in an answer. It was easy for him because he had the same type of phone and often sent texts.

THE DEED IS DONE.

A moment later came a reply. GOOD. NOW IT'S MY TURN TO HAVE FUN.

Olivia let out a little gasp.

"Oh God, I don't know who that is, but it makes me shudder to wonder what they think is fun."

The dog let out a whine as he took a few limping steps. Seth's leg was hurt, but not broken. There was also very little blood where the bullet had hit him.

Chief Ellison looked down at Ralston's body. The man was his own deputy, and yet, he was dressed like one of the neighborhood watch group. That told Ellison that someone had wanted to frame the group for his murder. But who? And why the hell was Ralston helping them?

"Dad?" Olivia called.

The chief stirred from his thoughts and saw that his daughter was pointing at an elderly man running toward them. It was one of their neighbors, a retired doctor named Hearns. The old man had a revolver in his hand, but it was still sheathed inside a holster.

"Hey there, John, Olivia. I heard the shooting and came running."

"Hi Doc, yeah, Olivia saved my life. That man tried to kill me."

The doctor was in his seventies, but still fit. When he squinted at Ralston's body, he looked upset.

"The Ralston boy? I know his family from when I practiced in Hartford. He tried to kill you? I thought he was a deputy?"

"Yes, he tried to kill me, and yeah, he was a deputy. Thanks to Olivia I'm still standing, but Ralston shot old Seth there in the leg."

The doctor called Seth over and the dog went to him.

"That's not too bad a wound, John. Why don't you let me take Seth in while you and Olivia handle this mess? I called your guys before leaving the house, and they're on the way."

Ellison thanked the doctor and watched as the old man led Seth away.

Olivia hugged her father. "Dad, what the hell is going on?"

"I don't know, honey, but as soon as a patrol car arrives to handle the scene, you and I are going to Gentry Court. Given the way that Ralston is dressed, I think the answer lies there in that cul-de-sac."

WHILE THE CHIEF WAS PLANNING TO VISIT TANNER'S neighborhood, someone else had just arrived there. It was Sara Blake.

Tanner had been sitting out on his front porch waiting for her to show, and he walked down the steps to greet her. He had just received a call from Alexa explaining what had happened at the hospital and knew she would be delayed in getting back to Killburry. Alexa had assured Tanner that her cut was minor, but he still worried and wouldn't be satisfied until he saw her again.

"Thanks for coming, Sara," Tanner said.

Sara grinned. "I still have to get used to you calling me by my first name. And look at this house, Tanner. You're becoming downright civilized."

"Only on the surface," Tanner said. "And remember, they know me as Tom Myers here."

They were leaving the driveway when Sara saw Josie step out onto the front porch of the house next door. Josie was staring at Sara with a scrutinizing gaze.

"I see you have nosy neighbors."

"That's Josie; I mentioned her yesterday."

"Oh, the neighborhood nympho?"

Tanner smiled. "That's one way to describe her."

"Who's that, Tom?" Josie said.

Tanner looked over and saw Josie with her arms crossed over her chest and glaring down at Sara.

"This is Sara, Josie."

"And does Alexa know about Sara? I know she's not home, Tom. I saw her leave earlier."

Tanner took Sara's hand and began walking up the steps with her. "What Alexa doesn't know won't hurt her, right?"

Josie opened her mouth in shock.

Tanner had reached his front door when Josie called to him.

"Tom!"

"Yes?"

Josie winked. "I'm next."

"Sorry, but you're too close to home."

Going along with the act, Sara reached up and touched Tanner on the cheek. "C'mon baby, I can't wait any longer."

"See you around, Josie," Tanner said.

He entered the house with Sara, and as he was shutting the door, he heard Josie call to him again.

"I'm gonna tell!"

He laughed along with Sara, then gestured toward the kitchen.

"As you heard, Alexa isn't back yet. I'll tell you the story over coffee, and she can give you a tour of the house some other time."

"I spent the morning at my own new home, the RV. It's stocked with food and I even stored some clothes there."

Sara gazed around the living room with an admiring eye. She looked at the few pictures on the mantle. There was one showing Tanner and Alexa, while the rest displayed Alexa with Emilio and Rodrigo, who Alexa had mentioned to Sara.

She turned and looked at Tanner. "No pictures of your family?"

"No. I don't have any," he said, which wasn't completely the truth. In New York, Laurel Ivy had possession of the lone photo she'd discovered that showed a young Tanner with his mother.

Sara walked over to him and stared up into his eyes. "You looked sad all of a sudden. I'm sorry, I didn't mean to bring up old memories."

"It's fine, but let's have that coffee, hmm?"

"All right, and Tanner, the house is beautiful. Did you two hire a decorator?"

"No, this was all chosen by Alexa. I paid for the house, but she furnished it."

"She has good taste," Sara said, "and in more ways than one."

15
YESTERDAY NEVER ENDS

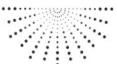

Mike Hodges ducked down behind a row of bushes and heard his knees crack loudly.

He was across the street from the home that had belonged to his nephew, Burt Hodges, but which now seemed to be the headquarters for a group of armed men. Three such men stood on the porch of the home with their weapons out in plain view.

There were also a number of large trucks scattered about the area, and men were moving furniture into the empty homes that Mike's nephew owned.

Mike had told Hodges to call him no matter what at noon each day. He had repeated the demand to Dexter the day before. When neither of his nephews made contact, or answered their phones, Mike decided to pay them a visit.

As he looked at the scene before him, he became certain that both of his nephews were dead.

More men poured out of Burt's house and they were also armed. Uncle Mike counted ten men. They were all dressed the same, in what looked like a blue uniform. He watched as they drove off in a pair of white vans.

He had seen the looks on their faces, the anticipatory glints in their eyes, and he knew that they were going off to cause mayhem. He had worn that same look often as a young man and had seen it reflected back in mirrors. Wherever they were headed, they expected to face little opposition and were looking forward to plunder.

Mike made his way around to the rear of the house he was at and sat on the back steps. He had brought along a gun, just in case. Now, he just had to find the nerve to use it.

Tanner finished telling Sara the story of Sean's attempt on Deke's life at the hospital.

"Are you sure Alexa is all right?" Sara said.

"She sounded good, but she had to have the cut on her arm bandaged, and she'll be giving a statement to the cops."

"If she hadn't been there, it sounds like Deke would be dead right now."

"Yes, and I guess this means that we'll have to reschedule our dinner."

Sara nodded in agreement but followed it with a little shrug. "We still have to eat, why don't the two of us go out?"

"Just you and me?"

Sara leaned across the table. "I'll tell Josie that I worked up an appetite in the bedroom."

Tanner smiled. "Why not? Like you said, we both have to eat anyway."

The sound of two vehicles coming to a screeching halt reached their ears. As Tanner cocked his head to listen, the squeak of doors opening on vehicles could be heard.

"What's going on?" Sara said.

As if in answer, the thunder of multiple rounds being fired simultaneously filled the air as scores of bullets ripped through the front of the house. Sara dived to the floor with her purse, which held her weapon. She then realized with horror and dismay that Tanner had frozen in place. She gazed up at him and saw that a haunted light had entered his eyes.

Tanner hit the floor and lay beside her an instant later, as the barrage of gunfire continued, and the sounds of destruction echoed throughout the home. His inaction had lasted only a moment, but Sara had seen the odd look in his eyes. It wasn't fear, but… something else.

What Sara had no way of knowing was that Tanner had lived through a similar situation before. That event had marked him in many ways, and he had been transported back in time to that day. Within that instant of inaction, in his mind's eye he had relived that horror, and had watched his family die all over again.

He lay beside her, whispering to himself. "This time I kill them all… this time I kill them all…"

"Tanner?" Sara said, as she took his hand.

"I'm good," he said in a hoarse voice, as he gripped her hand.

Tanner looked at Sara and saw the questions in her eyes, but he had neither the time nor inclination to answer them. "We have to get into the basement, follow me," he told her.

They crawled together toward a door on the right side of the room. The gunfire began to lose volume, then stopped altogether. However, it wasn't replaced by silence, but rather, there were the sounds of women screaming and children crying.

Gentry Court was under attack.

Outside Tanner's house, Adán was directing the five men with him, including Choa. They were all dressed like cops without the badges and other paraphernalia such as police radios. They also wore ski masks and latex gloves.

The six men had shredded the front of Tanner's house by firing nearly four hundred rounds of ammo. Spent magazines and brass shells littered the ground at their feet.

Adán told Choa to stay with him and then sent the other men to enter Tanner's house and confirm that he was dead. The men carried a battering ram that had the logo of the Killburry police on it.

Four of his other men had entered the homes of the neighborhood watch group, who were also believed to be vigilantes. Adán knew that the husbands weren't at home during the middle of a workday, but they would be taught a valuable lesson before he returned to the other side of the park.

Anna, Louise, Tina, and Josie were all herded from their homes at gunpoint. The women had their children with them, all but Josie, who was childless. Other neighbors peeked out at the scene. Adán told his men to herd the children toward one of the neighbors who had a child of her own.

When Anna protested and held on to her baby, Adán changed her mind.

"If you want these children to live, you'll let them go."

The children were all handed off after that, and passed to the other neighbor, who disappeared with the crying brood back into her house.

When Adán noticed that one of his men had a fat lip sticking out from his ski mask, he asked what happened.

The injured man pointed at Josie, whose own bottom lip was bleeding.

"The little bitch caught me with a hell of a kick. I was glad that I had the gun."

Adán spoke to the man, as well as the others who had rounded up the women. "Stay with them while we make sure that Myers is dead," Adán said, and he and Choa moved toward Tanner's house.

In the basement of Tanner's home, Sara gazed in shock at what Tanner was showing her.

"A tunnel? Why is there a tunnel under your house?"

"Just be glad that it's here," Tanner said, and handed Sara a flashlight.

"Where does it lead to?"

"There's a shed in my back yard. We'll emerge inside it, and I have weapons hidden there too."

"Lead the way," Sara said, and was surprised to see Tanner head off to another corner of the basement. "Where are you going?"

Tanner didn't answer, and up above there came the sound of someone knocking the front door off its hinges.

Moments later, Adán and Choa entered Tanner's home and Adán shouted for his men.

A voice answered back from the basement. "We're down here! There's a tunnel!"

Choa called Adán over to the mantle and pointed out the picture of Tanner and Alexa.

"That's Myers."

Adán smashed the picture frame, tore off the side with Alexa's face, and used a phone to take a picture of the photo.

"I sent that to Chang. If Myers gets away, we'll have the whole Brotherhood chasing his ass."

Adán and Choa left the fireplace and rushed down to the basement. There was an entrance in a wall that had been hidden behind shelving. The shelving was pushed aside, and Adán called to his men.

"Do you see Myers?"

"No, but there's no light coming from the other end. He must still be in the tunnel. Wait a minute, I feel something."

Adán had taken two strides into the tunnel when it collapsed. Choa yanked his cousin backwards and hit the floor, as the screams of the other men reverberated throughout the basement.

Choa and Adán got to their feet and choked on the dust that filled the air. When he could find his voice, Adán called to his men, but received no answer.

Choa grabbed his cousin's arm. "We have to go!"

Adán silently agreed and rushed up the basement steps, with Choa following. Their feet slipped along the way, as the wooden steps were coated with a fine layer of dirt from the tunnel collapse.

They were headed out of the house when Adán punched a wall. The act was fueled by frustration and fury. Adán had just lost four men. They were all friends that he had known for years. Instead of walking outside, Adán headed for the kitchen.

"Adán?" Choa said.

Adán turned on a burner on the stove and a flame rose up high.

"I'm going to burn Myers' house to the ground, Choa, right to the fucking ground."

16
BURNED!

Chief Ellison switched on the lights and siren as he headed toward the cul-de-sac where Tanner lived. He had been going there anyway, but then received calls that armed men were in the area and shooting up a house.

Olivia was seated beside her father with her rifle between her legs and was wearing a bulletproof vest. Two other patrol cars followed behind.

When Ellison's radio alerted him to a call, he learned that all of the members of the neighborhood watch had been accounted for. That included Ted Anderson, who had to be tracked down at a house he was showing to a prospective buyer.

"There's just one odd thing, Chief. None of the men can get their wives on the phone."

The chief thanked his dispatcher and drove faster.

"Dad, one of the callers said that Tom Myers' house was the one being shot up. What do you think that means?"

"If it's as bad as they described… I think he might be dead."

Olivia let out a sad sigh, as she gripped her rifle tighter.

ADÁN AND CHOA WALKED OUT THE FRONT DOOR OF Tanner's home with tendrils of smoke swirling around them. They had gone upstairs and set the bedroom on fire, then ignited several other rooms.

They rejoined their men, who were still holding the women at gunpoint, as the crackling sound of a growing fire filled the air. One of the men asked Adán where the other men were.

"They're dead. Myers tried to escape in a tunnel, and it collapsed on him and the others."

"What do we do with these women?" Choa asked.

Adán surprised everyone by taking off his mask. "We waste these bitches, that's what we do."

Upon hearing those words, Anna, Louise, Tina, and Josie huddled together. Louise began whispering a prayer as the men took several steps back and raised their weapons.

Automatic fire ripped the air, mixing with screams, and eclipsed the sound of the growing inferno that had been Tanner's house.

DEKE SMILED WHEN HE SAW THAT ALEXA HAD RETURNED TO his hospital room. She wore a bandage around her left forearm and was clutching a bottle of pills.

Deke started laughing. "Only you would use a cactus as an edged weapon, Alexa."

Alexa laughed along as she reached out and took Deke's hand, to give it a squeeze.

"It was the only sharp thing available and so I used it, but I guess I owe you a gift."

"Just having you here is gift enough. And oh yeah, you just happened to save my life. Thank you."

"You're welcome," Alexa said. She released Deke's hand and took a seat next to the bed. "I have to drive to the police station when I leave here and give a statement. They're saying that the man who came here to kill you was blinded in one eye. I think they're also hoping to hold him responsible for the attack at Burke last week."

"Good, that sounds like he'll be going away for a long time," Deke said.

"What are your doctors saying, Deke?"

"The news is good now that I beat that lung infection. I might get out of here by next week."

"That soon?"

"Yeah, I'll be a little weak, but my strength will return in time."

"Are you going back to Burke?"

Deke shook his head. "No, Alexa, I think it's time I moved on. I had a lot of time to think while I was in here."

"Oh, I'll miss you, Deke, really."

Deke stared at her for a moment. "Tell me the truth, why did you want to see me the day of the attack?"

Alexa made an apologetic face. "I was going to say that we couldn't be friends anymore."

"Because I want more than friendship, right?"

"Yes, am I wrong?"

"Hell no, you're not wrong. I only hold back because you're already with someone. Now that you two have a house and are settled… I see that my hope that things might change were a waste of time. I'm sorry too, if I ever made you feel uncomfortable."

Alexa patted Deke on the arm. "You haven't, and I'll miss you as a friend."

"I should have cut things off between us earlier," Deke said. "When two people want different things out of life, there's no hope for happiness. That's just the way life works."

Alexa winced at hearing Deke's words. She and Tanner wanted different things, but they would make it work, she told herself. She and Tanner would be the exception.

There seemed to be nothing else to say, so Alexa said goodbye to Deke. As she walked back to her car, she was filled with a sense of loss for the end of a friendship and found herself wiping at tears.

DOZENS OF ROUNDS RIPPED APART ADÁN AND HIS MEN, causing the marauders to scream out in pain and surprise.

It was Tanner and Sara. The tunnel that Adán's men entered was a dead end. It had been built as a trap and designed to collapse. Tanner and Sara had escaped from Tanner's home in the real tunnel he had built beneath the stairs, and which he sealed tight after entering.

They emerged from the tunnel inside his tool shed, where he kept a hidden gun safe. Inside the safe were a pair of AR-15's that Tanner had modified to fire at full auto. Those rifles were now being put to good use to end the siege of Gentry Court.

Adán and Choa were positioned on the far side of the line of men. They had both been hit once, but their wounds hadn't disabled them. Although, they were off balance and spattered with blood from their dying comrades.

Both men swiveled to their right to return fire. They

never got the chance. Tanner had reloaded, slapped the charging handle, and sent a burst into the torsos of Choa and Adán. Sara reloaded an instant later, set her AR to semi-auto, and sent three-round blasts into each of the men.

The women of Gentry Court moaned in relief as they recovered from their close call, but then Josie pointed at Tanner's home.

"Oh Tom… your house."

Tanner turned, looked at his home, and knew that it was lost.

A gentle hand touched him on the cheek. It was Sara.

"I'm sorry, but at least no one is in there."

Tanner headed toward the woods even as he loaded a new magazine into the AR.

"Where are you going?" Sara said.

"To finish this. Those men were from Hodges. I recognized one of them."

Sara followed. "We'll do it together."

Tanner bit back his objections. Sara had nearly died as well, and she was as capable as anyone he'd ever known.

They marched through the woods and would circle the park to emerge on the other side, while unaware that they were headed toward incredible odds.

Tanner and Sara disappeared among the trees, and police sirens grew louder, as Chief Ellison rushed to the scene.

He was far too late.

17

YOU CAN TAKE THE BOY OUT OF THE PRISON...

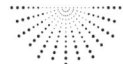

"It's a damn army," Mike Hodges whispered to himself.

He was back to hiding behind the bushes and watching the houses across the street, his nephew's house, and the homes surrounding it. Carloads of men were showing up, hard men.

Mike looked down at his old Colt revolver and knew he'd never get revenge for the loss of his two nephews.

A hand appeared, a female hand that snatched the gun away, as another hand, a male hand, clamped over his mouth. Mike felt himself being dragged backwards around to the rear of the house and driven to the ground. As a knee pressed against the small of his back, Mike heard a familiar voice whisper.

"What the hell is going on here, Hodges?"

Mike turned his head and saw a beautiful woman staring down at him with a pair of cold blue eyes. When he turned his head a little more, he saw the man he knew as Tom Myers.

"It's the Brotherhood, Myers; they call themselves the

Brotherhood. My nephew tried to join them… but they killed him. The sons of bitches killed Burt and Dexter."

Tanner helped Mike to stand and told Sara to stay put and keep an eye on him.

"Where are you going?" Sara said.

"To look around. I have to know what we're up against."

Sara shook her head. "You've seen them. There's too many."

"There are never too many, just the lack of a plan. Don't worry; I won't engage them."

"Then why risk it?"

Tanner sighed. "I have to look for someone, actually two people, they probably got caught in the middle of this mess. If I'm not back in ten minutes, leave."

Sara opened her mouth to protest, but Tanner had already disappeared behind the bushes.

THERE WAS A STREAM THAT RAN BY THE REAR OF HODGES' home. It was a tributary that miles away flowed into the river that ran by Chief Ellison's house. The gangbanger named Reo had taken Pete and Rocco there to kill them and dump them in the water. The order came from Chang, who didn't want anyone around who wasn't a part of the Brotherhood.

Reo's buddy, Dominic, kept looking back at the house. "Reo, we should just slit their throats and drop them in the water. Plus, this shit ain't right. We're out of prison now, we can go find some women."

Reo smiled and slapped a hand across Rocco's naked ass. He had secured the boy's arms around a tree and yanked Rocco's pants down.

"Look at this shit, Dom. Why let it go to waste?"

"Leave my little brother alone!" Pete yelled, and received a hard back-handed slap from Dominic. Dominic then pointed at Rocco.

"If you're gonna fuck him, then fuck him before Chang sees us."

Reo unzipped, unbuckled, and let his pants drop to the ground. As he reached out to grab Rocco by the hips, he heard Dominic make a weird noise, like a gurgled cry. That was followed by the sound of something splashing.

Reo turned his head to look over at his friend and saw Dominic falling forward with his throat slit wide open. Standing behind Dominic was a man with a bloody knife, and he was moving toward Reo fast.

"Shit!"

Reo took two steps toward his gun, which was laying on a nearby tree stump. He tripped over his own pants. In his rush to grab a weapon, he'd forgotten that his pants were unfastened.

Tanner ran over and gave Reo a vicious kick to the side of the head, as Pete rushed over to free his brother from the tree.

After Tanner's kick stunned him, Reo had moaned and rolled over onto his back. His eyes fluttered open just in time to see the boot headed for his throat.

TANNER CRUSHED THE LIFE OUT OF REO WHILE KEEPING HIS head turned to watch the rear of the house. He could hear voices coming from inside and was glad the blinds were down. But if anyone came out, he would have to use the gun, which would alert everyone.

He had been listening at a window on the side of the

house when he heard Pete yell at Reo and went to investigate.

Something slammed into Tanner just as he removed his foot from Reo's throat. It was Rocco. The boy was shaking violently, as tears ran down his cheeks. Rocco wrapped his arms around Tanner and spoke through sobs.

"You saved me, Tom Myers, you saved me."

Tanner went to push the boy off, but instead, he patted him on the back.

"It's okay, kid. They can't hurt you anymore."

With his face still pressed against Tanner's chest, Rocco nodded. "Thank you, Tom Myers, thank you."

Tanner spoke to Pete. "We have to get out of here and we have to do it quietly. Take your brother's hand and follow me."

SARA HAD REMAINED WAITING WITH MIKE DESPITE THE FACT that Tanner had been gone for more than twenty minutes. When she saw that he had company, she pointed at Pete and Rocco.

"Who are they?"

"They're recent acquaintances."

Mike pointed toward the park. "My car is in there. Let's get out of here before we're spotted."

Tanner stared at Hodges for a second, then he told Sara to give Mike back his gun.

They reached the car quickly and Mike asked Tanner where he wanted to go. After a moment's thought, Tanner gave him directions to the lake property gifted to him and Sara by Conrad Burke.

As they drove along, Sara whispered to Tanner. "You

have to contact Alexa. She can't just ride up to the house and learn what happened to it."

"I know," Tanner said, "and I am not looking forward to it. Alexa loved that house."

Across the park, what had been his home was sending a column of smoke into the evening sky.

18
CHEEKY

Chief Ellison leaned back against his police car and tried to make sense of everything he'd learned so far. He was in front of Tanner's house, which was a burnt hulk that still smoldered in places.

He had eleven dead bodies to deal with, including one of his own deputies. And while Deputy Ralston had been dressed like one of the men who made up the neighborhood watch group, the other ten men had been dressed like cops, in blue pants and shirts. Six of the men had been cut down in the street by gunfire, while four other men were discovered in the ruins of Tom Myers' house. To top it all off, those four were located inside a false tunnel built in Myers' basement.

Tom Myers was missing, as was a woman named Sara Blake, whose car was found parked in Myers' driveway.

Although eyewitness accounts varied widely, Myers and the Blake woman were said to be the ones who shot down the six men. It was reported that they did so to save the wives of the neighborhood watch group.

When Chief Ellison saw the dead men, he had

recognized Choa and was planning to speak to Burt Hodges. One of the other men, Adán Mora, had possession of a cheap cell phone that had sent the text to Tim Ralston. The message that asked Ralston if he had killed the chief. This kind of muscle and ballsy nerve was above and beyond Burt Hodges, the chief was sure of it, but Hodges was his only link to the dead men.

However, when Ellison sent a deputy to pick Hodges up for questioning, he learned that Hodges was gone and that a corporation he had never heard of now owned all of Hodges' properties. The deputy also informed the chief that there were numerous men with firearms in the area. When the deputy asked one of the men if he had a carry permit, the man was able to produce one, although he looked like a stone-cold thug and was covered in gang tattoos.

Ellison stirred from his thoughts as his daughter walked over to stand beside him. Olivia should have been placed on desk duty since she had been involved in a shooting, but the chief needed her. Not only was she a good officer, but after the day's events, she was the only one of his people he trusted. Rules and propriety could wait.

Olivia gestured at the scene before them. "Dad, what the hell is going on today?"

Ellison placed an arm around his daughter's shoulders and pulled her close. It was an act of affection he normally wouldn't display while they were both in uniform, but the day was not an average day.

"I don't know what's going on, baby, but I do know that we need help. Get in the car. We're going to see the man."

"The man? You mean the mayor?"

"No, I mean the CEO of Silicon City. This is his town, if he wants to keep it, he'll have to fight for it."

Ellison drove out of Gentry Court and went off to see the man.

∼

AT THE LAKE PROPERTY, SARA HAD SETTLED MIKE, PETE, and Rocco inside her RV, while she waited with Tanner inside his own RV.

Alexa had finished at the police station but had been called back to the hospital. She also told Tanner that she would stop to grab a meal. Tanner hadn't informed Alexa about the house being destroyed. It was not news that she should hear over the phone.

Tanner sat behind the wheel of the massive RV and looked out the windshield for signs of Alexa's headlights. It wasn't quite dark yet, but soon would be. Sara sat beside Tanner in the passenger seat and decided to talk about the elephant in the room.

"What was that back at the house, that delayed reaction you had?"

Tanner remained silent for a moment, but then sighed. What had happened during the assault on his home couldn't be ignored, and to his surprise, he realized he trusted Sara enough to talk to her about it.

"I froze. No excuses, but there was a reason for it."

"Yes?"

"When I was sixteen, Alonso Alvarado came to my family's home with dozens of men and opened fire on it. I... I was the only one to survive."

"Oh, good Lord," Sara whispered as she moved to the edge of her seat. "It's no wonder you despised the man. I knew you had no family, but I figured it was due to natural causes or accident, not... wholesale slaughter."

"Alexa went through something similar, but even more

horrific, at Alvarado's hands. It's one reason we're so close. When the gunfire began, and I heard the rounds splintering the walls, it was like I was back there." Tanner gave his head a slight shake as he recalled his instant of inaction. "To freeze like that, that cannot happen, not to me, not to a Tanner."

A gentle kiss touched his cheek, startling him, and he turned his head to find Sara smiling at him.

"You are the toughest, bravest, and deadliest man that ever lived, but you're still a man, still human. Don't beat yourself up over this."

"My delay in reacting could have cost us both our lives."

Sara stood. "Yes, but it didn't, and now we have to find a way to make the Brotherhood pay. Come to my RV after you've talked to Alexa. We need to make a plan."

"We?" Tanner said.

"Yes, we; I may not be a Tanner, but I can be of assistance to you, and Mike Hodges says that he has an idea that might help."

"Fine. I'll be there later, and Alexa should be back soon."

"Good luck with that. Facing the Brotherhood might be easier."

"Yes, Alexa will not be pleased. She really loved that house."

"Tanner?"

"Yeah?"

"The tunnel, you built that didn't you?"

"Yes, Sara."

"Thank God you did, and about the house, you can always rebuild."

"That will be up to Alexa."

Sara said goodbye and stepped outside, where she

headed for her own RV upon the path that connected them.

Three minutes later, Alexa arrived and came down along the new section of road to park near the RV.

Tanner rose from his seat and steeled himself to break the terrible news.

19

DIVERGENT DESIRES

CHANG SCOWLED AS HE STARED DOWN AT THE BODIES OF the gangbangers Reo and Dominic.

Earlier, he had learned that his best recruiter and his team of enforcers had been slaughtered, and that the assassination of the Chief of Police had been foiled.

Chang had no idea how the chief had survived and assumed that he was a tough man to kill. He knew for certain that Adán and his men would not be easy to best, but it appeared as if one man was responsible for their deaths; a man named Tom Myers.

Chang wondered if Myers had also killed Reo and Dominic, if so, he had fled afterwards. Myers must have seen the growing number of armed men entering the area and decided to run away. Still, would a man who was capable of killing Adán and his men be intimidated?

Chang turned and spoke to one of his lieutenants. He instructed the man to increase the number of men who would be guarding the house where the Brotherhood Council would be holding their meeting the following day

It was the house behind them, the one that was once Burt Hodges' home.

The meeting had to go smoothly, and no one, not Tom Myers or anyone else would ruin it. Once the meeting was over, and the men had settled into their new homes, then, Myers could be hunted down and killed.

Chang had to assume that Myers would warn Joe Pullo, and so the battle for control of New York would have to begin within days. Forewarned or not, Chang was confident that the Brotherhood would have victory over the Giacconi Family.

Chang pointed at the bodies of Reo and Dominic and told his men to drag them farther away and dump them in the stream. There was a section nearby where the stream widened on its way to join up with the river. With luck, the corpses might never surface. Chang also told the men to dispose of any other trash they might find.

Tomorrow's meeting had to go well, as Chang planned to solidify his position as leader of the Brotherhood Council. By acquiring Hodges' homes as a base, he had done just that.

Chang went back inside the house. There was still much work to do.

ALEXA ROSE FROM THE BED INSIDE THE RV AND WIPED AT the last of her tears. Hearing about the destruction of her home had devastated her, but she was more upset by Tanner having suffered such a close brush with death. She walked over to him and fell into his arms, while laying her head on his chest.

"Why does violence seem to follow you?"

"You had your own violent event today, remember? I had nothing to do with that."

"Didn't you? That was all part of the attack on the Burke campus, and we're only involved with Burke because you take contracts. Violence will be a part of our lives for as long as you remain a Tanner."

Tanner released her and sat on the RV's semicircular sofa.

"We're back to that, hmm?"

"We're not back to that discussion, we've never really had it. If you remain a Tanner our lives will never be normal, and I want normal, Cody. I want to be Mrs. Cody Parker, I want to own a ranch, and I want to raise your children."

"And I want to remain a Tanner. I want to take contracts and I want to be the best at what I do. Where does that leave us, Alexa?"

Alexa sat beside Tanner and took his face in her hands. "This Brotherhood organization, they destroyed our home but not us. Leave here, Cody, leave Killburry, leave the USA, and come to Mexico. We could be so happy there; I know that we could."

"You're not listening to me, Alexa. I'm a Tanner and I want to stay a Tanner. And as far as the Brotherhood, there's not even a question that they'll pay for destroying our house. They'll pay, and they'll pay in blood."

Alexa stood in a rush. "I don't care if they pay! Insurance will cover the cost and we can find another house, but Cody, I'm so sick to death of violence, of revenge, of hatred. I just want to live a peaceful life and raise good children. Is that too much to ask?"

Tanner took a deep breath and let out a heavy sigh. "It's not too much to ask... I just think that you're asking it of the wrong man. And Alexa, I do love you. Don't doubt that."

Alexa wiped at fresh tears. "I'm going to take a shower and go to bed early."

"I'll be along later. I'm going to Sara's RV to make plans concerning the Brotherhood."

Alexa threw her hands up in the air. "Go! Do what you want, but Goddamn you, Cody, do not get killed. I love you too. I couldn't stand to see you come to harm."

Tanner walked over and gently touched the bandage on Alexa's arm. "Speaking of that, are you sure the cut's not bad? I saw that you had several bottles of pills. Why so many?"

"Oh, one is a painkiller, but the rest are just vitamins. The doctor thought that I needed to take supplements. I also received a tetanus shot."

"I see, and does your arm hurt?"

"It did earlier, but the pills helped," Alexa said.

Tanner leaned in and kissed her. "I'll try to be back soon. Sara realized that we wouldn't have any clothes, and she left you a new jogging outfit that she bought yesterday. There's a washer and dryer, but they're tiny. We also have no food here, so we'll have to shop."

Alexa looked around. "It's not a home, but it beats a hotel room."

"We can find a new home, or rebuild if you'd like?"

"I just told you what I wanted. I want to start over in Mexico."

"Yes Alexa, I heard you."

Tanner went to the door and walked out. There was nothing left to say.

20

HE DON'T PLAY

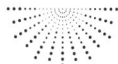

"A DRONE?" SARA ASKED MIKE HODGES. "YOU MEAN LIKE a toy?"

"It's a toy, yeah, but it's also got a camera and can give us a bird's eye view of the area around my nephew's house."

Tanner looked at the video of a drone that was playing on Sara's phone. They were all seated around the fold-down table in her RV. Tanner had driven Pete and Rocco up to the shack in Alexa's car and settled them in there for the night.

He would have to find someplace for the teens to go that was safe, but the shack would do for now. After leaving the shack, he returned to Sara's RV and began making plans to strike back against the Brotherhood.

"A drone might work," Tanner said, "but I'd want to use it for more than surveillance. If I know where the men are, I can either kill or avoid them. An eye in the sky would aid in that, but I can't spend my time looking down at a screen."

Sara gestured at Mike. "If he flies the drone, I can

communicate to you where the men are and tell you what's around the next corner. We'll just have to rig up an earpiece for you."

Mike had learned that Tom Myers was actually Tanner, but he had never heard of Tanner. He looked confused while swiveling his attention between Sara and Tanner.

"Wait a minute, are you really thinking about going up against all these guys alone?"

"He can handle it, Mike," Sara said. "Although Tanner, shouldn't you give Pullo a call?"

"I'll let Joe know about the Brotherhood threat once I've crippled them, otherwise, it'll just start a war in Killburry."

"Killing a few of their men won't cripple the Brotherhood," Mike said. "Burt made it sound like these guys had an army, and there are hundreds of them there already."

"Yes, and their generals are having a meeting tomorrow in Killburry. I overheard some men discussing it when I went to get Pete and Rocco."

Sara smiled. "You figure that if you cut off the head, the snake might die?"

"Exactly, this council of theirs, if I kill them all, the Brotherhood may break up and dissolve back into its different gangs. It's actually surprising that they've come together at all."

"What do we need beside a drone and a way to communicate?" Sara asked.

"You and I will go shopping early in the morning, then join up with Mike in Killburry. He'll need time to become used to the new drone we'll buy."

"We could use my grandson's," Mike said.

"How good is the camera?" Tanner asked.

"It's okay, but I see your point. An upgrade would be better."

"We need something with a good camera that can hover quietly," Sara said. "And you still have those two near-silent guns that Deke made for you, Tanner. But can you think of anything else?"

"A water gun, one of the big ones."

Sara wrinkled her brow in confusion.

"Why would you need that?"

"I'm going to fight fire with fire. The drone will help me move about safely, and the quiet guns will make it possible to kill the guards without alerting anyone inside the house."

"And the water gun?" Sara said.

"Will contain gasoline, enough to burn that house to the ground with everyone in it. The Brotherhood destroyed my home. I plan to return the favor, in spades."

Mike sat back and stared at Tanner. "You play rough."

Tanner shook his head. "No Mike, I don't play."

THE CEO OF SILICON CITY LIVED IN A PENTHOUSE apartment that sat atop the corporation's main complex in Killburry. The man traveled a great deal for business, but Chief Ellison had gotten lucky and found that he was in residence. After a short wait, the chief and his daughter were escorted into the penthouse by one of the CEO's security people.

The CEO was named Martin Anders. Every time the chief met with him, he was struck by how young the man was. Anders was thirty three but looked even younger. The sandy-haired genius had given birth to Silicon City as a website while still in high school. Fifteen years later, he was on his way to becoming a billionaire.

In some ways, Anders was like Chang. Both men had gathered together disparate groups within their fields of interest and brought them together to form a greater whole. Silicon City was the techie version of the Brotherhood.

Anders met the chief with a warm smile and an offered hand, but he was actually eyeing Olivia.

"Chief, it's good to see you again."

Ellison introduced his daughter and Anders extended his hand again. "Deputy Ellison, it's nice to meet you."

Olivia smiled at Anders and was surprised when he blushed slightly while shaking her hand in greeting. The man might be highly successful, but he was still a shy, nerdy college kid at heart. Olivia found it endearing.

They sat, and Anders asked his live-in housekeeper, a middle-aged woman, to bring them coffee. When the chief told Anders that coffee wasn't necessary, Anders told the housekeeper goodnight and moved the meeting out onto his balcony.

"You only ask to see me when there's trouble, Chief. Does it have anything to do with that fire that was over by the park?"

"Yes sir, and it is bad news."

The chief went on to tell Anders about the attack on Gentry Court, the attempt on his life, and the horde of men now living in the homes formerly owned by Burt Hodges. When he went into detail about the circumstances surrounding each event, Anders smiled at Olivia.

"You saved your father's life, and from such a distance. I'm impressed."

Olivia shrugged. "I've always been good with a rifle."

Anders gestured about the balcony. "I sit out here

often. I guess I better not make you angry; I'd be a sitting duck."

Olivia smiled. "You have nothing to worry about; I only shoot bad guys."

Anders smiled back at her. The chief took in the exchange and wasn't sure if Anders was hitting on his daughter or not. If so, why not? They were both single, and hell, the man was filthy rich. Still, Ellison cleared his throat to get things back on track.

"Anyway, with eleven deaths in one day, the news will pick up on this, and we'll definitely see a huge spike in our crime statistics," the chief said.

Anders shook his head sadly. "How can I help? Does your department need more equipment?"

"No sir, you could give us a tank and we couldn't handle this. What we need is federal muscle. There are a pair of FBI agents on their way here, but I need more than that, and you have the influence to make that happen."

Anders stared down at the floor for a moment, but then stood and took a phone from his pocket.

"Please excuse me for a few moments," Anders said, and disappeared back into the penthouse.

While they waited, the chief made a call of his own, to check on Seth, the dog. His neighbor, Dr. Hearns, assured the chief that Seth was fine. Hearns said that he had already fed Seth and taken him for a walk along with his own dog, which was a boxer.

"He limps a little, but that leg will heal quickly, and I've treated the wound," Dr. Hearns said.

Ellison thanked him and was telling Olivia about Seth when Anders returned and handed him a slip of paper.

"That's the name of the head agent who will be leading the task force looking into today's events. She'll be at the station tomorrow at eight a.m."

Ellison looked down at the paper. "Task force? You have an FBI task force coming here?"

Anders looked worried. "Is that enough help, or should I have asked for more?"

Olivia laughed. "A task force is awesome, Mr. Anders, and thank you."

"Good, and Deputy Ellison, please call me Martin."

"Martin? All right, and I'm Olivia, Martin."

As they were leaving, Anders asked Olivia for her phone number.

"I'd like to call you… for updates."

Olivia smiled and gave him her number.

WHILE THEY WERE RIDING DOWN IN THE ELEVATOR, THE chief made a prediction.

"I bet Anders calls you for more than news about the task force."

"That's fine by me; the man is cute."

"And rich. You have my permission to marry him."

Olivia laughed and felt the tension of the day slip away.

21

TOOTHLESS AND BLIND

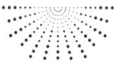

EARLY THE NEXT MORNING, TANNER WENT SHOPPING WITH Sara, while Pete and Rocco tagged along. The siblings had basically been evicted by the Brotherhood, and so Tanner bought them clothing and other essentials.

Alexa had decided to stay behind and sleep late. She was depressed about losing her house. Tanner couldn't blame her. While the house hadn't meant as much to him as it did to her, living there had grown on him.

Tanner had spent most of his adult life moving from one temporary residence to another. He had also spent those years going from one woman to another. Having passed the last few weeks with the same woman inside the same home was a new experience for him, but far from unpleasant. Perhaps it was his age, he thought. He was in his mid-thirties and had done more living than most men do in a lifetime.

Hotel room service was a beautiful thing, and lovely young ladies eager to please were even nicer. However, he had risen the day before and sat out on his deck drinking coffee while waiting for a woman he loved to rise from their bed and join him. Tanner had liked that, was discovering that he looked forward to those simple pleasures, and far more than he ever thought he would. He wanted more of them. He could have them for the asking if he gave up being a Tanner. However, that was something he would never do. He loved being a Tanner. But Alexa's offer was tempting, while the thought of losing her fostered bleakness.

～

Pete and Rocco smiled with delight every time Tanner said yes to something they wanted, but he made sure they understood that nothing was free.

"You'll earn everything I'm buying you. Miss Blake and I are letting you live in the shack and you can work as caretakers. Neither one of us will be staying in the RV's full-time and you two can make sure that no one breaks into them."

"You're gonna let us live at the lake, Tom Myers?" Rocco asked.

"That's right, kid. Do you want to?"

Rocco grinned. "I love swimming and fishing, so yeah."

Sara smiled at Rocco. She had spent time with him on the previous evening and found him to be an innocent. That was a rare thing in this world. She was also impressed that Tanner had taken the time and risked himself to rescue Rocco and his brother. Tanner could be cold as ice at times, but he wasn't heartless. After learning about the trauma he'd suffered through while losing his family, Sara felt as if she understood him better. The simple truth was, the more she learned about the man, the more she liked him.

"We still have to buy the drone and a water gun," Sara

said. "But then I think we're good. I stopped in the electronics department and found an earpiece that you can wear while I direct you around the Brotherhood's men."

"I'm more concerned about the drone. It needs to be as quiet as possible. If it's spotted, someone will shoot at it."

THE TOY STORE WAS HUGE AND CARRIED SOME BASIC fishing equipment, so Tanner hooked up Pete and Rocco with poles and lures. When they saw that Tanner was buying a water gun, they insisted on having two of their own. Tanner let them grab what they wanted, but he put his foot down and removed the cans of Silly String that Rocco sat in the cart.

"No more of that," he said. "It took me an hour to get it all out of my hair."

Sara gave them a questioning look, but Tanner waved her off.

The boys also got a dart board, and at Sara's urging, bicycles, to be delivered. They were the type that had a big basket at the rear to transport things.

"They'll need a way to get to the store and the laundromat," Sara said.

"I can drive a car," Pete said. "And so can Rocco... a little."

"I'm not buying you a car, kid," Tanner said.

They settled on a drone that appeared to meet their needs. It was supposed to be quiet, while the camera had good definition. Sara and Mike Hodges would be operating the drone from the nearby park, so the range of the radio signal was more than sufficient.

Tanner returned to the RV to find that Alexa was up and dressed. After putting away the bag of food he had bought, Tanner told her he had to leave for Killburry.

He had expected Alexa to argue and to ask him to please let his battle with the Brotherhood go, but instead, she kissed him and told him to be careful.

"I'll be back later," Tanner said.

Alexa just nodded at him, but then something occurred to her. "Are you using my car? If you do, I'll be stuck here."

"No, Sara rented a car while we were out."

"Good."

"Are you going anywhere?"

"I don't know, but I just didn't want to be stuck here."

"You're not stuck here, Alexa," Tanner said, and the double meaning of those words weren't lost on him, or her.

"I'll be here when you get back."

"Good," Tanner said, and then he left the RV. His destination: Killburry, and war.

Mike Hodges let out a whistle of appreciation when he saw the drone Tanner and Sara had purchased. It had a much wider wingspan than the one he was used to, but he found that the controls were similar.

By noon, Mike could maneuver the machine wherever he wanted it to go and was enjoying the speed of the drone. Although bigger and heavier, it was also faster than the toy his grandson played with.

While Mike had been getting used to the new drone, Sara and Tanner had worked on the communication devices. Tanner could hear Sara's voice in his ear even over a great distance, as well as communicate back to her.

Mike complained about the weather, which was cloudy and windy, with the threat of rain in the forecast.

"I got the hang of this thing real quick, but it would be much harder for anyone to spot if it were bright and sunny."

The two of them gathered around Mike as he sent the drone on a recon mission over his late nephew's house. There were men on all sides of the home, and Sara wondered how Tanner could approach it without being spotted.

"If you cut through the other yards, the men on the porch will see you," she said.

Tanner pointed to the stream that ran behind the house. "I'll wade along in that until I'm at the back of the house. There are trees there that will block the view of the men on the porch."

Sara shook her head. "That will get you there, but you'll still have five men to kill, and you'll have to do it without alerting the men stationed on both sides of the house."

"I'll have to be patient after leaving the water and wait until one of them comes to me. Once I eliminate the first man, I'll only have to kill four at once."

"Why would one of the men go into the trees back there?" Sara asked.

Mike answered her. "They'll go there to take a leak. It's easier than going inside the house. But Tanner, four guys is still a lot. You can't miss a single time and they'll have to be fatal shots."

"I know, Mike; I can do it."

Sara touched Tanner on the arm. "I could come with you."

"No, I need you here to read the scene and let me know what's around the next corner. Mike could do it, but I'd rather he'd just concentrate on flying the drone, especially with the wind picking up the way it is."

"All right, but if you get into trouble, I'll have your back."

"No, Sara. Stay here no matter what happens. If we do lose communication, I'll find my way out of there, but not until I give the Brotherhood a taste of what they dished out yesterday. Those bastards are going to pay for burning Alexa's house."

"An eye for an eye, a tooth for a tooth?" Mike said.

"Toothless and blind will be more like it," Tanner said.

Sara pointed at the view the drone was transmitting. They had watched the arrival earlier of over a dozen important men. The men seemed important because each of them arrived with two bodyguards. Tanner assumed that they were council members and saw they were being led around the area as if on a tour. The outing appeared to be over as everyone was entering Burt Hodges' house.

"It looks like the Brotherhood Council is going inside for their meeting," Sara said.

Tanner put on the backpack that held his weapons and ammo, including the water gun and the container of gasoline.

"That's my signal."

"Be careful, Tanner," Sara said, "and come back in one piece."

Tanner inserted the audio device into his ear. "You'll be with me every step of the way."

"Give 'em hell, Tanner," Mike said.

Tanner sent him a nod and headed off to do what he did best—kill.

22
WHOOSH!

CHANG ACCEPTED THE PRAISE THAT CAME HIS WAY FROM most of the members of the Brotherhood Council, who were gathered around a conference table.

His acquisition of Hodges' properties was pivotal in establishing a base for their organization. In Hartford, the different groups that comprised the Brotherhood were scattered about the city by necessity, but now, now they could be united.

"It is from here that we will launch our attacks on New York and Boston," Chang said. "And before long, we will control the entire east coast."

One of Chang's dissenters was a tall black man named Williamson. Williamson controlled a militant group with ties to New York City. He stood and spoke to Chang.

"New York will know we're coming, Chang. Your boy Adán and his crew got their asses killed by a damn suburbanite. I also heard that the man knows Joe Pullo. If that's true, we won't have to go to Pullo, Pullo will come here."

Chang forced a smile onto his face. It was something

he was good at. Williamson was always a thorn in his side, but he knew how to handle him.

"Pullo may be alerted, but what does it matter? We are strong, we are many, and we will overrun New York and crush the Giacconi Family. Don't forget, Williamson, Pullo's organization is still recovering from their earlier wars."

"I'm not forgetting shit, but Pullo is no joke. Plus, he's got Tanner on his side, and that son of a bitch is a damn killing machine."

Chang's smiled widened, as if to dismiss Williamson's assertions. "You worry too much. Tanner is just one man."

"So was this guy who whacked Adán and his crew. And what about him? He still has to be handled."

Chang held up a finger as if to say, "Wait a second," he then fiddled with his phone and sent a photo to the flat screen monitor that had been hung over the fireplace. It was the photo of Tanner and Alexa with Alexa missing from it. Adán had sent Chang a picture of it the day before, then died soon after at Tanner and Sara's hands.

"Adán sent me this picture of Myers. I suggest we distribute it to—"

"Oh, hell no," Williamson said, as he rushed over to the monitor to stare at it. "This is no damn Tom Myers. This dude is Tanner. I met him once."

"Tanner?" Chang said. "Are you certain?"

"Look at those eyes, who the hell could forget him? The dude is smiling in the picture and I still feel threatened."

One of the other council members stood. His name was Roberto. He ran a gang that had over a hundred men in it.

"If this Myers is really Tanner, then Joe Pullo already

has his eye on this town. That means that troops from New York City could be headed here right now."

"Forget, Pullo," Williamson said. "We need to worry about Tanner. He's already here."

Conversations broke out around the table as the council members discussed their options; Chang watched it all with a growing sense of frustration. This was not how he had planned for the day to go. Unfortunately, things were about to get worse.

A FAINTLY ORANGE STREAM OF LIQUID ARCED THROUGH THE air as Tanner slit the throat of a gangbanger who had been taking a leak. The urine mixed with the blood from the man's jugular and flowed down the short hill and into the stream.

Tanner left the man lying on his back and gasping for air his lungs would never receive, as his windpipe had also been severed.

Two men stood on the porch, while two more sat on the back steps and smoked. When one of the men on the porch decided to sit, Tanner figured he would never have a better chance and took aim at the seated man while leaning around a tree.

Tanner was using the guns designed by Deke Mercer. They were damn near silent when used with their special ammo, and Tanner placed a round just below the nose of the seated man.

The man grunted as his head snapped backwards, but the other man on the porch ignored him. He had heard the gun, and quiet or not, it put him on alert.

"Did you guys hear "

The second round ended the man's query, as well as his

life. As the body tumbled onto the floor of the porch, the other two men snapped their heads his way. One of those heads exploded in the following instant, while the man beside him took two in the back of the neck.

That man flopped noisily on the stairs before dying, and Tanner asked Sara if the men on the side of the house had heard the commotion.

"No, you're good, Tanner. The men on both sides of the house are busy talking to each other, and nice shooting."

"Thanks, but I've a long way to go. I'll kill the men on my left next."

"How do you plan to kill the two men on that side?" Sara said. "They're staying close to the front, and there are another five men out there."

"Bait, and once they bite, I'll have them."

Tanner removed money from his side pocket and dropped it on the ground. The day was cloudy, but there was wind as well. The money moved along the side of the house sluggishly, since it was still wet from Tanner's trek in the stream. The bills caught at the base of the small shrubs at the side of the house, where they flapped in the growing breeze. It took more than a minute, but one of the men stationed at the side of the home noticed the movement and began walking toward the rear.

"They're headed your way, big spender," Sara said.

Tanner smiled but readied himself for action. As the men grew nearer, he heard them talking.

"It's money, man, look, a ten."

"Screw that, I see a twenty," the other guard said, he was leaning over to pick it up when Tanner shot him in the crown of his head, then fired a pair of well-placed shots into his buddy, who was also bent over.

Tanner left them where they lay and headed toward

the front, but not before using the water gun to send streams of gasoline over the rear of the house. He laid down some along the side, and also wet the wood on the windowsills.

"How are you going to take out the guys up front, Tanner?" Mike asked. He spoke loud in order to be heard through Sara's microphone.

"It's time to start the fire."

"You mean…?"

"That's right," Tanner said. He flicked on a disposable lighter as he moved along and locked the flame on high. The water gun could shoot liquid over thirty feet. Tanner walked around the side of the house while firing a stream of gasoline.

AT THE POLICE STATION, THE FBI WAS GEARING UP TO SEND more than eighty men and women at the Brotherhood. Chief Ellison learned that the FBI had already formed the task force that was in his town. It had been based in Hartford and had tracked the activities of the Brotherhood for months.

The carry permit that his officer had seen the day before was legit but had been obtained through graft. The FBI could prove that, as well as other charges. Given the Brotherhood's recent activities, it had been decided to take them down.

What had been a task force, became a joint task force of FBI agents, state police, and officers from the Killburry police department. Those officers included the chief and his daughter.

Once warrants were issued, Ellison and Olivia climbed

into a black SUV with the head FBI agent, and drove toward Burt Hodges' house.

The chief smiled at his daughter. "So much for our quiet little town."

Olivia smiled back, but she felt a flutter of fear as well.

THE FIRST MAN TO SPOT TANNER WAS A WHITE supremacist with a gleaming shaved head. He opened his mouth to shout and Tanner filled it with gasoline. The other four men were also sprayed to one degree or another, and Tanner tossed the lighter, even as one of the men fired at him.

A loud *WHOOSH!* erupted amid the men's screams, as overhead, the drone lost sight of Tanner as a gust of wind pushed it out of position. The last sight Sara had seen was that of Tanner falling to the ground.

"Damn the wind!" Mike said. "Hold on, Sara. I'll put her back in the right spot."

Sara shouted into her microphone. "Tanner! Are you all right? The two men from the other side must be headed your way." There was no answer, just the screams from the men who were set ablaze. "Tanner, the fire is set. You have to get out of there."

"Look!" Mike said, as he pointed at the monitor. He had taken the drone higher to try to avoid the wind currents, and the view showed dozens of men pouring from the other houses. Having heard the gunshot, they were all running toward the home that was now surrounded by flames on all sides.

One of the men from the porch had jumped down and ran into the alley, headed for the stream in back, but he fell before getting there as the flames blinded him. He set the alley side of the home on fire, as he came in contact with the trash that was heaped there. The trash consisted of the belongings of Burt and Dexter, including their clothing. Had it not been dumped there, the men inside might have found a way out.

Dozens of armed men converged on the home, but there was no sign of Tanner, and no answer to Sara's pleas.

"Tanner, say something. Are you injured? Tanner?"

There was still no answer, but then Mike zoomed in to a bit of color that had caught his eye. It was the water gun. It was melted and still ablaze. Lying beside it was a body, and it too was burned.

Sara pointed at the right side of the figure's smoldering scalp, where something white could be seen lying on the ground.

"Can you zoom in closer?" she asked Mike.

He did so, and Sara gasped. "No."

"What is it? What is that thing?"

"It's Tanner's earpiece."

"Oh shit, I'm sorry, Sara."

Sara lowered herself to the grass, as a range of emotions passed through her, one of them shocked her, as she realized how much she cared for Tanner.

Tanner? Yes, this was Tanner, she reminded herself. Sara stood and pointed at the screen. "Pull back again, we have to find him. We have to know if he needs help."

"But I thought that was him we just saw?"

Sara shook her head. "No, not Tanner. He's alive."

Mike sighed. "Whatever you say, Sara."

Sara wiped away tears. "He's alive. Tanner is alive."

23

OBSCENE FIRE AND OBSCENE RAIN

Chang caught the flicker of flames outside the windows of the makeshift conference room only an instant before the screaming began.

The members of the Brotherhood Council all jumped to their feet at once. Williamson, who was already standing near the door, opened it to shout orders to all the different bodyguards who were awaiting their masters.

"Go see what all that damn screaming is about."

That was when the single shot sounded off as one of the men on the porch fired his weapon at Tanner. The bodyguards all rushed down the short hallway to the door. When one of them opened it, he revealed a scene from hell. The entire front of the house was ablaze, and men were on fire and writhing in agony.

"There's a damn fire!" the guard said uselessly, as the truth of his statement was in plain view for everyone to see. He had turned to talk, and never saw the flaming form coming at him. The figure knocked him down and set him on fire as well.

He pushed the dying man off and ripped his burning

shirt from his body, to toss it away. The shirt landed at the base of a wall and set the curtains ablaze. Meanwhile, the burning man who had run inside had ignited the carpet. The material was designed to be flame resistant, but the man had tracked gasoline into the house, which fueled the blaze.

"We have to get the fuck out of here!" someone cried.

What followed was a mad rush as the Brotherhood Council fled about the home looking for a way out. There was none, there were only flames, and the smoke that grew thicker with each second that passed.

Someone thought of the roof, and the pull-down stairs that allowed access to the attic were located and engaged. The stairs were old and folded down on a pair of weak hinges. They were not meant to be used by several men at once.

Six men made it up into the attic before the stairs collapsed and broke into pieces. Among the men who had made it into the attic were Chang and Williamson. Those still below in the hallway struggled to climb through the hole left behind but were succumbing to the smoke one by one. Had they worked together, most of them would have made it.

The attic was filling with smoke as well, but Williamson shoved open a window and climbed outside. He was followed by the others, including Chang.

All six men made it up to one side of the slanted roof and gazed over at a safe haven, the roof of the home across from them.

"We have to jump," Williamson said.

One of the other men pointed. "It's too far; we'll fall."

Another man pushed by the pointing man, climbed up higher, and stood with bended knees while trying to maintain his balance.

"It's jump or die," the man said, and he took off running.

He died.

His leap was a yard short and he fell thirty-six feet to the ground below, while screaming.

The scream ended abruptly.

"Not another fire," Ellison moaned.

He and the others had seen the smoke as they grew closer to the area. They were growing close and Ellison called for the fire department.

Olivia took her father's hand. "Do you think it's Tom Myers getting revenge?"

"I don't know, but he might be denied."

"What do you mean?" Olivia said, but then she heard it. The sky, which had looked threatening all morning, was making good on its threat, and a steady rain began to fall.

Sara huddled miserably beside Mike as the rain began soaking them to the skin. She was about to give up hope again, and seek shelter, when she saw a figure moving around behind the homes.

"Zoom in on that house right there. I just saw someone running."

"All right, but I have to bring the drone back soon or this rain will ruin it. The wind is getting rough too."

"There!" Sara said, as the figure darted into the open and along to the next house. It was Tanner, and he was holding a makeshift torch and setting the other homes on fire.

"He's alive!" Sara said, as she hugged Mike.

"You were right, and it looks like he's not done causing mayhem."

They kept the camera on Tanner until the rain finally doused the torch. By the time that occurred, he had already set a dozen homes ablaze.

When Tanner headed back toward the park, Sara told Mike to bring the drone in. She looked like a wet mop with her hair hanging down, but a smile lit her face.

Tanner was alive, and that fact made her happier than imagining him dead ever had.

THE CROWD OF THUGS GATHERED IN THE STREET WERE watching the blaze, several of them had their heads tilted back to catch the sudden rain in their mouths. One of them spotted Tanner out of the corner of his eye, and then noticed that there was smoke drifting out of some of the other homes.

The man was about to cry out and go in pursuit when the sound of sirens blared. The FBI and the police had approached silently, but only after first dropping agents and officers out to move into position. When the police vehicles came in sight of the crowd, they hit the lights and sirens.

The men tried to scatter but found that there were already law enforcement agents moving in with their weapons drawn.

Chief Ellison leveled his shotgun at a biker holding a gun. "Drop your weapon and get down on the ground!"

The man hesitated, but then fell to his knees. Olivia had come up behind him and kicked his feet out from under him.

"Hands behind your back!" she said, and father and daughter went to work rounding up the members of the Brotherhood.

ON THE ROOF, CHANG AND THE OTHERS HAD GRINNED when the rain began, but then realized that it wasn't the boon they had hoped it would be. The house below them was too far gone for a simple bout of heavy rain to extinguish the flames consuming it.

Meanwhile, the roofing tiles had become slick, while the heat of the fire was intense and had buckled in one section of the roof. There were flames and smoke escaping from the hole.

Chang wiped the sweat and rain from his eyes and came to the same conclusion that Williamson had.

"We have to jump. There's no other way."

"We'll fall," one of the other men said, like Chang, he was Chinese, and an original member of the Brotherhood.

The man next to him gritted his teeth as he spoke. "I'd rather fall than burn."

The man looked to his left, where his friend stood. They were from the same gang of thieves.

"On three," the other man said.

When the count was done, the pair took off. The first man missed the roof, but just barely. The other man landed on its edge, but the rain-slick surface made it too difficult to keep his footing. He tumbled backwards and followed his friend to the ground. One of the two men had survived the fall and was screaming in agony.

Chang's friend covered his ears and walked a few steps There was a groaning noise, the sound of wood splintering, then the roof opened with a spout of flame and swallowed the man.

"Shit!" Williamson said.

"I'm jumping!" Chang said.

Williamson moved back near Chang as both men tried to get as much sprinting room as they could. It was difficult because of the roof's slant and the slickness caused by the rain. The two men sent each other a nod, then they ran for the edge.

Both of them made it onto the other roof, but as the other man had done, they slid backwards. Unlike the other man, Williamson and Chang fell forward. Then clawed at the roof tiles for purchase. Their slide continued, but then stopped, as their feet slammed into a section of the home's rain gutter. Amid laughter, they realized that they had made it.

Their rejoicing ended abruptly. The rain gutter had given way on one side. The sudden shift threw Williamson off balance, and he reached out a hand to Chang.

Chang kept his hands firmly attached to the edge of the roofing tiles he still held onto and watched with dispassion as Williamson tumbled away. Williamson's fall ended the screaming coming from the man below, and Chang assumed that Williamson had fallen on the man.

It took over a minute, but Chang clawed his way onto the new roof and sat with his back against a chimney. Each of his feet touched one side of the roof, which was as slanted as the home he'd escaped from.

The rain was chilling Chang on the left side, even as the fire was roasting him on the right, but he was alive. He smiled when he realized that he was the only member of the Brotherhood Council to survive.

Down below, the street soldiers of the Brotherhood were being herded into vans and police vehicles. Chang was undaunted by the scene. He would see that those men were freed and then would gather them together again. The Brotherhood was wounded, but not destroyed, and when it rose from the ashes, he alone would be in charge.

Chang had no doubt that Tanner was behind the fire. Adán had burnt the man's home to the ground and he had returned the favor. Chang vowed to himself that he would destroy Tanner, Pullo, and anyone else who stood in his way. He would teach them the folly of daring to cross him, and the Brotherhood would grow stronger.

A fire engine appeared and fought its way to the burning house. Chang took off his white dress shirt and began waving it in the air, to attract attention and summon help.

When Chang first heard the noise, he thought it was an insect, but it grew too loud for that. He swiveled his head about, thinking it was the noise from some sort of rescue equipment. He never saw it coming until it hit him in the face.

It was the drone, and the force of the impact made Chang lose his balance. He let out a scream as he slid face first off the roof and down into the driveway, where his skull shattered upon impact with one of Williamson's knees.

IN THE PARK, TANNER HANDED THE REMOTE CONTROL FOR the drone back to Mike.

"That was fun. Thanks for letting me take it for a spin."

Mike laughed, then appeared surprised as he looked at the monitor. "Holy crap, the thing is still flying. I'll bring it in for a landing."

Tanner turned around and saw that Sara was soaked to the skin.

"We need to get you somewhere dry," he said.

"I'm good, and you two are as wet as I am."

"Being wet from the stream saved me. One of the men on the porch shot the water gun from my hand. The gas splashed onto me, but my clothes were too wet to ignite."

"You lost your earpiece too… it concerned us."

Tanner pointed toward Gentry Court, where the remains of his home sat. "I'd invite you both in to get dry, but I don't think I have a roof anymore."

Sara beamed at Tanner.

He cocked his head. "What's with the smile?"

"I'm just happy."

"Well good, I'm happy that you're happy."

Mike brought the drone in for a landing. "Let's get out of here. We'll go to my daughter's house; it's not far and we can all get dry."

"That drone idea made things much easier, Mike," Tanner said. "I was glad to have your help."

"Thanks. I did it for Burt and Dexter."

TANNER AND SARA FOLLOWED MIKE AS TANNER DROVE Sara's rental. The rain had stopped as suddenly as it had begun, and the sun was fighting its way past the clouds.

"Tanner."

"Yeah?"

"Do you think the Brotherhood is done?"

"I don't know, but they won't be bothering Joe anytime soon."

"Speaking of New York, I received a call from Jacques Durand. He said he may be in New York soon."

"Did he have any news about Maurice Scallato?"

"No, but there's a possibility he'll have an offer for you."

"A contract?"

"Yes."

"I hope the target is interesting, and I've been meaning to go back to New York City soon."

"Manhattan holds a lot of bad memories for me."

"Really? Or is it more like a mixed bag?"

Sara thought about it and gave a little nod. "I guess you're right; it is a mixed bag."

"Nothing is all bad, Sara."

She gave Tanner a sideways glance and smiled to herself.

"Yes, I've figured that out."

24

NO COMMENT

Tanner returned to the RV to find that Alexa had been shopping. The cabinets were full of food, and she had already cooked something for dinner on the tiny stove.

Alexa hugged him fiercely when he walked in the door and asked him why he was wearing a matching sweatshirt and sweatpants. He explained that they were given to him by Mike Hodges, after his own clothes were ruined by gasoline.

"Gasoline? Did someone try to set you on fire?"

"No, just the opposite, and the Brotherhood are no longer a problem."

"You killed them all?"

"I killed their leaders, which is just as good."

Alexa settled on the sofa and Tanner followed and sat beside her.

"Does this mean that you can never go back to Killbury, or use the Tom Myers identity again?"

"Sara is working on that. She had to leave her car behind yesterday, knowing Chief Ellison, he's aware that the vehicle belongs to her. He must be looking for both of us."

"I want to see our house. I want to see what's become of it."

Tanner kissed her lightly on the mouth. "Maybe you shouldn't."

"Was it that bad?"

"I didn't mention this part yesterday, but… the men that attacked, they shot the home up before setting it on fire. There are hundreds of bullet holes, unless it burned to the ground."

Alexa turned toward him and searched his face. "Was it like when your family was killed?"

Tanner nodded, and Alexa hugged him. "Oh Cody, that must have been horrible for you."

"Yes," Tanner said, then, he cleared his throat. "We'll rebuild. I'll contact an architect and you can design the home the way you want it."

Alexa shook her head. "I don't want that, and you know it."

Tanner fell back against the sofa. "You want us to move to Mexico and you want me to give up being a Tanner."

"Yes, and yes, I know it's incredibly selfish of me, but it's what I want, and I'm tired of pretending that I don't."

"I want to continue doing what I do, Alexa, and I want you by my side. How do those two worlds meet?"

They stared at each other, both of them knowing the answer to that question.

Alexa stood, reached down, and when Tanner took her hand, she tugged, urging him to his feet.

After a kiss, she smiled.

"Whatever happens, I love you."

"And I love you," Tanner said.

They disappeared into the bedroom, to put their differences on hold, for just a little while.

∽

Tanner and Sara walked into the Killburry police station the following afternoon.

The deputies on duty looked up from their desks as conversations ceased. Olivia was at the coffeemaker and had just pushed the BREW button. When she spotted Tanner, she crossed her arms over her chest and glared at him, then, she looked Sara over.

"Mr. Myers, I would say that it's nice to see that you're well, but I have a feeling that you're very capable of taking care of yourself."

"As are you," Tanner said. "I read about your heroics in the paper."

Olivia looked at Sara again. "You're Sara Blake, yes?"

"Yes," Sara said.

"My father would like to speak with both of you. Please follow me."

The chief's door was open and so they just walked in with Olivia leading the way. Olivia stood beside her father's chair as she had done previously, but her gaze was more serious than it had been on Tanner's last visit.

The chief leaned back in his seat and let out a weary sigh. "Mr. Tom Myers, or whoever you are, and Miss Blake, to what do I owe this visit?"

"I understand that you want to see me, Chief," Tanner said.

"I did, and I had a hell of a lot of questions for you too, that is, until I received a call at home last night. The caller, a Mr. Lawson, made it quite clear that you and Miss Blake were hands off. He said it nicely, but the bottom line is that I have no authority to even question you about the events of the last few days."

Olivia stepped forward. "Did you kill those men, Mr. Myers? The ones that burnt your house down, and the men who took over Burt Hodges home, did you kill them as well?"

Tanner looked at the Chief and saw that he was smiling.

"Mr. Lawson never talked to my daughter."

Sara stood to leave, but Tanner remained seated.

"Chief, Deputy Ellison, any actions I might have taken were in self-defense."

"Self-defense?" Olivia said, with a tone of incredulity. "That fire at Burt Hodges' house killed dozens of men."

"These men that were killed, were they innocents?"

Chief Ellison chuckled. "They were the scum of the earth. More than a few of them had done hard time."

"I see; it sounds like the town is better off without them."

The chief jabbed a finger at Tanner. "You don't get to decide that. There are laws, and there are reasons for those laws. What if someone inside that house was innocent?"

"Then they would have perished along with the guilty, as is often the case in this world. Those are God's rules, not mine."

Olivia leaned over the desk and stared at Tanner. "Who are you, really?"

Tanner stood. "I'm a tax-paying citizen of the town of Killburry, Deputy, and maybe I'll see you around sometime."

Tanner was heading out the door with Sara when the chief called to him. "Contact your insurance company; something has to be done about your home."

"Yeah, I'm headed there next."

"Oh, and Myers, about the vigilantes, it's those wives, isn't it? They're the real neighborhood watch."

Tanner smiled, said, "No comment," and went off to Gentry Court.

∾

Josie ran off her porch and into Tanner's arms when she saw him step out of a taxi with Sara.

Tanner was surprised by the show of affection, and he recognized it as such.

Josie ended her embrace with a squeeze and smiled up at Tanner. "That hug wasn't a come-on, it was gratitude. You saved my life, Tom; hell, you saved all of us."

"It was my pleasure, but Sara helped."

Josie looked over at Sara. Sara was at her car, the one she had to abandon after killing Adán and his men. She was looking at the windshield, which had become filthy because of the soot and ash of the house fire. She would drive it back to the lake property, while Tanner drove his jeep, which was equally dirty.

"You're not really sleeping with Sara, are you?"

"No."

"I didn't think so. I'm as hot as she is, and if you can resist me, you can resist anybody."

Tanner smiled. "Your logic is sound."

Anna, Louise, and Tina joined them and gave their thanks to Tanner and Sara. They were surprised that "Tom" had avoided jail time, but they all had given statements saying that Tanner and Sara had acted to save their lives. When they asked about Alexa, Tanner told them that he didn't know when she would come back to the neighborhood. He assured them that he would relay to Alexa that the ladies wanted to see her.

He also let them know that Chief Ellison was on to them. The women all shrugged. They would continue their vigilante activities if they saw a problem but said they would be more careful.

A representative from the insurance company appeared and told Tanner the obvious, the house was a total loss. When Josie asked Tanner his plans, he told her the truth. He didn't know.

"Maybe we'll rebuild and live here again, or maybe we'll sell it. It all depends on Alexa."

The women waved to him as he drove off, and Tanner wondered if he'd ever see them again.

25
GUARDIAN ANGEL

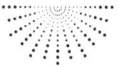

HIRAM SCHWARTZ KEPT REMINDING HIMSELF THAT HE HAD nothing to be afraid of, even as the gang of thugs approached him inside the exercise yard at the county jail.

His Uncle Abraham had promised him that he would be protected, and Hiram believed that his uncle was a man of his word. Hiram also knew that his Uncle Abraham was an embezzler.

Over a period of five months, ending just a few weeks earlier, Uncle Abraham had siphoned funds out of an account, then cleverly hid his tracks. Hiram had stumbled upon the truth by accident and was flabbergasted.

Hiram uncovered the thievery a year after he went to work at the same company where his uncle had been employed for decades. Having only recently graduated from college at the time, Hiram had been thrilled to get a position as an assistant accountant, and doubly excited to be working near his uncle, whom he loved.

When Hiram confronted his uncle about the missing funds, the man confessed, citing an out of control gambling habit as the reason for his thievery. Uncle

Abraham said he was getting help with his addiction, and that was why the thieving had already ceased prior to Hiram's discovery.

Hiram was proud of his uncle. The man had made mistakes, yes, but he was willing to face his shortcomings and was getting the help he needed.

However, the missing money was another story, and Hiram assured his uncle that the shortage of funds would be uncovered by Hiram's superiors, and that there was no way to avoid it in the long run. That was when Uncle Abraham shocked Hiram.

"My boy, I need you to take the blame for these thefts."

"Me? But Uncle Abraham, why would I do that?"

"Think about it Hiram. I am respected here and have many friends throughout the community. Were I to be associated with such low behavior, it would be a disgrace that I could never recover from. Your aunt and your cousins would share in that shame as well. Also, my retirement would be in jeopardy, and I might even be expected to drain funds from my accounts to pay back the money I stole. But you, boy, why you're a young man, and young men make mistakes. You'll have a lifetime to bounce back from this, and I will do my best to help you."

Hiram felt sick. He saw the logic, of course, and he wanted to help out, but jail? The thought of going to jail frightened Hiram. He was a small man, and a Jew. Small Jewish men did not do well in prison environments. Hiram was certain of that.

However, after more persuasion by his uncle, Hiram agreed to take the fall. Uncle Abraham consulted with a friend who was a well-known attorney, and the man agreed to defend Hiram. The lawyer predicted that Hiram would do no more than six months in the county jail and then be on probation. The money, over twenty grand, would of course, have to be paid back in full.

Hiram thought he could do six months in jail. Yes, he could endure it to help out his beloved Uncle Abraham, but he did have one request. He wanted his uncle's word that nothing bad would befall him while he was inside the jail.

"As you say, Uncle, you're a respected man and have many friends, surely you could have someone of influence see that no harm befalls me. I'll do the time and remain silent about the truth, but I couldn't stand to be brutalized. I've heard horror stories about what goes on in prison."

Uncle Abraham had laid a hand on Hiram's shoulder and stared into his eyes. "You have my word, boy. No harm will befall you. Why it will be as if you have a guardian angel watching over you. If anyone dares to lay a hand on you, they will be smote by your protector."

"Smote?"

"Smitten, destroyed, no one will harm you, my boy. You have my word."

Hiram had smiled, and feeling assured that he would suffer no harm, he took the blame for his uncle's thievery.

Uncle Abraham was not only a thief, but a practiced liar as well. He had no gambling habit. The money had gone to a blonde stripper named Honey Potts. If Honey hadn't left for California to make her fortune in the porn business, Uncle Abraham would have kept embezzling to keep her happy.

Hiram's gullibility was a blessing, and Uncle Abraham was only too happy to sacrifice the young fool. And as far as Hiram being protected by a guardian angel, it was pure fantasy.

Uncle Abraham had no doubt that Hiram would emerge from his ordeal in jail the worse for wear, but much wiser. And isn't that one of an uncle's duties, to help his nephew attain wisdom?

∽

Hiram swallowed hard as the group of eight men made their way over to him. They all looked huge to Hiram, who was only five-foot-five.

One of the men even wore an eye patch, and the others seemed to be egging him on. Hiram, who had only been inside for two days, was still certain that the man with the eye patch was new to the jail. Hiram thought it wasn't very likely that he would have missed noticing him. That's when Hiram knew he was meant to be some sort of initiation test for the man with the eye patch, and when he spotted the tattoo of a swastika on the man's wrist, he knew he was in serious trouble.

∽

Sean smiled at Hiram Schwartz. He was going to have fun beating the crap out of the little Jew. He had to be careful though, he didn't want to do anything that would add more time to his sentence.

His lawyer was a Jew, and damn if those Jews weren't great at law. The man had successfully argued with the DA. He had made the state drop any charges against him that had to do with his group's attack on the Burke Corporate Campus.

And why not? They had no proof that he was there. And yes, he did bring a knife into a hospital, and yeah, he made a threat to Deke Mercer. But that was it, that was all he was charged with, and the Jew lawyer said he would likely do only ninety days in county.

FIRE WITH FIRE

Hell, Sean could do ninety days in a comfortable cell without breaking a sweat. Then, once he got out, he would make a point of tracking down the spick bitch that made him lose his left eye. After he made her suffer and die, he'd track down Deke Mercer and finish what he'd started.

But first, it was time to become one of the boys of the white brotherhood inside the county jail, and that meant beating the snot out of Hiram Schwartz.

SEAN GAVE HIRAM A SHOVE, THEN APPEARED SHOCKED BY the nerve the little man displayed.

"You don't want to do that," Hiram said.

Hiram's voice squeaked as he spoke, but he reminded himself of the words his Uncle Abraham had spoken. He had a guardian angel, and if anyone tried to harm him, they would be smote. Or was it smitten? Well, it wouldn't go well for them.

Sean laughed. "What are you gonna do, Jew boy, are you gonna kick my ass?"

Hiram shook his head. "No, I don't have to do a thing. I have a guardian angel."

Sean and the other white supremacists laughed at Hiram. Sean was especially amused.

"Hey Jew boy, I'm gonna fuck you up, then I'm gonna sell you to the queers for a pack of smokes. What's your guardian angel have to say about that?"

Hiram had begun to shake. He wanted to believe, but the thought of being beaten, and then to be handed over to men who would—No! His Uncle Abraham would not lie. He was protected, and the man with the eye patch was tempting fate.

"If you hit me, you'll be sorry," Hiram said. "My guardian angel will smite you."

"Smite?" One of the men said, and the group laughed again. When their laughter died down, Sean shook his head sadly at Hiram.

"Jew boy, I'm gonna show you some smite right now."

Sean reared back a fist but never threw the punch. A hole appeared between his eyes, followed by the back of his head ripping open from a massive exit wound. Blood and brains sprayed his companions and made them stumble backwards with awe lighting their faces.

Sean's body fell to the ground, and the men looked across the splayed form at Hiram.

Hiram had a look of wonder in his eyes. He turned, grinned like a fiend, and flashed a thumbs up sign at the heavens. He then uttered words that sent chills down the other men's spines.

"Thanks, guardian angel!"

A moment later, and the yard erupted in chaos as the correction officers rushed the men back to their cells.

HALF A MILE AWAY, TANNER WAS SMIRKING. HE HAD looked through his scope at Hiram and saw the small man flash him a thumbs up.

The man's reaction amused him. He hadn't killed Sean for Hiram, but rather, to protect Alexa.

Tanner removed the sound suppressor from the end of his rifle's barrel. It was a custom model designed and built for him by Deke Mercer and it was even better than military grade. He had heard the fired shot but doubted it had carried to the exercise yard.

He was on the roof of an abandoned apartment house

that was scheduled to be demolished soon. Although no one else thought the building still held usefulness, Tanner had found it to be very handy. It had given him a direct line of sight into the exercise yard of the county jail, while also allowing him to avoid being in view of the guard towers.

Tanner had the rifle broken down in no time and loaded into a gym bag. A careful climb down the rickety metal stairs of the building's weathered fire escape and he was back on the ground.

He returned home to the RV an hour later to find Alexa perusing real estate listings in Mexico. In particular, ranch land.

"I'm just looking out of curiosity," she explained.

"Right," Tanner said.

He might lose her if she left him, but he'd never lose her to scum like the neo-Nazi Sean. Tanner kissed her, sat beside her, and wondered how much longer he'd have her in his life.

26
ANYTHING IS IMPOSSIBLE

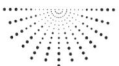

Alexa left Tanner two weeks later.

They had both come to the inescapable conclusion that they wouldn't last as a couple and decided to separate before one of them became resentful of the other.

Alexa had returned to Mexico, to her father's house. However, thanks to the check she received from Conrad Burke in appreciation of her bravery, she would have enough to buy a ranch.

Tanner said he would visit someday, but he wasn't sure if he were lying or not. Alexa would find someone else, he was certain of that, and seeing her with another man was not something he needed to experience.

Things were quiet at Burke, at least where the wet works program was concerned, and Jacques Durand's trip to New York City had been pushed back indefinitely. Any offer of work from Durand's contacts had also been put on hold.

With nothing to do and no desire or energy to do it, Tanner sat inside his RV and drank. He was depressed. It was a rare thing for him, but not unknown, and he had last suffered through a bout of it after walking away from Laurel Ivy years ago.

This time the woman walked out on him, but the pain was the same, and the sense of loss, the absence of Alexa, it all felt as physical to him as the amputation of a limb.

While drinking, he would damn himself for getting too close to Alexa, for letting her in, when he knew from experience that love only brought pain. Still, he wouldn't go back and change a thing, and he had loved every moment he'd spent with her. If only they hadn't been so different, but things were as they were, and he was who he was.

SARA RETURNED TO THE LAKE AFTER LEAVING HER SISTER'S wedding, and to her surprise, Tanner was seated out on the dock. She was glad to see he had finally left his trailer, and hoped it meant that he was getting over Alexa.

The floating dock had been placed in the lake while Alexa was still around. Sara also had one installed on her side of the lake. There were boats as well; two small row boats, and Pete and Rocco were using one to fish.

Sara waved to the boys as she walked over to join Tanner. She was still wearing a blue chiffon dress, her maid of honor dress, along with its matching shoes.

Tanner needed a shave and looked to Sara as if he'd lost some weight.

Sara removed the shoes, lowered herself beside Tanner, and placed her toes in the water.

Tanner looked her over. "Why are you so dressed up?"

"I just came from Jenny's wedding. She and Jake are off on their honeymoon."

"Oh, where did they go?"

Sara didn't answer, and Tanner looked at her.

"What?"

Sara had a pained expression on her face. "They're in Mexico, Cancún."

Tanner sighed. "I'm not a basket case, Sara. I won't tear up at the slightest mention of Mexico."

"I didn't think you would, but to talk about Mexico just felt… I don't know, insensitive?"

"You had a visitor today, Deke Mercer."

"Deke came here? But I just saw him last night at the apartment house. Did he say what he wanted?"

"It was just an excuse to see Alexa; he still thought she was here."

"Yes, I never said anything to him about her leaving."

"I told him that she had gone back to Mexico for good, and he let me know that he was going down there to see her."

Sara shielded her eyes and made a show of looking around the shoreline.

"Where did you put it, Tanner?"

Tanner gave her a confused look. "Where did I put what?"

Sara grinned. "Deke's grave, I want to pay my respects."

Tanner smiled. It was the first one he'd had on his face since Alexa left.

"He's still above ground. And hell, maybe they'll make a go of it. Alexa could do worse than Deke Mercer."

Sara reached over and gave his hand a squeeze, then released it. "She's already done better than Deke; she just didn't appreciate that fact."

Out on the lake, cheers rose from the boys, as Rocco reeled in a good size trout.

"It looks like we'll be having fish tonight," Tanner said. "I'll grill it; would you care to join us?"

"Yes, I just have to change out of this dress, and I'll make a salad to go with the fish."

"Good. By the way, I'll be leaving here tomorrow."

"Where are you going? To New York?"

Tanner stood up, then leaned over to grab his shoes. "New York City can wait. I'm going to hunt down Maurice Scallato and I'm going to kill him. I should have done it already."

"How will you find him?"

"I don't know."

Sara stood and walked close to Tanner. "Let me come with you; I can help."

"No, this is something I'll do alone."

"But you don't have to, and the two of us will have a better chance of finding him."

Sara expected Tanner to say no again, but instead, he nodded.

"You're right, if there's one thing I've learned these last few months, it's that I don't have to do everything alone."

Sara moved closer. "That's right, you're not alone."

Tanner stared down at her. "I'll be damned."

"What?"

"I think we're friends."

Sara laughed. "Yes, we are friends now, and all we had to do was survive each other."

Tanner touched her on the cheek. "That was no easy feat. We damn near killed each other a few times."

They continued staring into each other's eyes, as Tanner's touch became a caress. Sara closed her eyes, as if awaiting a kiss, but then she felt Tanner move away. When she opened her eyes, she saw that he was looking at her strangely.

"I should get that grill going," Tanner said.

"Yes, and I'll make a salad."

Tanner walked off the dock and headed up toward the shack. Sara watched him, and there was a small smile playing on her lips.

She had stopped denying her feelings for Tanner since she believed he had died while attacking the Brotherhood. She felt something for the man. It wasn't love, but it was affection, strong affection. What Tanner might feel for her, if anything, was as great a mystery to Sara as was the future.

If she and Tanner would ever be more than friends, God only knew.

Sara scooped up her shoes and left the dock while whistling. One thing was for certain, with Alexa gone, anything was possible.

Tanner watched Sara walk back to her car and vowed to stay away from alcohol for a while. He must still be a little drunk because he had nearly kissed her, an act that would have upset her and ruined their budding friendship.

Friendship? Yes, they were friends, and more, because he trusted her, and trust wasn't something he gave easily.

It was a certainty that Sara Blake would never sleep with him. Friendship was one thing; intimacy was something else altogether. Her hatred toward him may have ceased to exist, but Tanner was sure she would never think of him that way.

Tanner smiled to himself.

Him and Sara Blake?

No, some things just weren't possible.

Tanner attached a propane tank to the barbecue grill. As he worked, he thought of ways to track down Maurice Scallato. It was time to make the hunter the hunted.

Scallato would die.

TANNER RETURNS!

TO KILL A KILLER - BOOK 16

AFTERWORD

Thank you,

REMINGTON KANE

JOIN MY INNER CIRCLE

You'll receive FREE books, such as,

SLAY BELLS – A TANNER NOVEL – BOOK 0
TAKEN! ALPHABET SERIES – 26 ORIGINAL TAKEN! TALES

Also – Exclusive short stories featuring TANNER, along with other books.

TO BECOME AN INNER CIRCLE MEMBER, GO TO:
http://remingtonkane.com/mailing-list/

The Young Guns Series in order

YOUNG GUNS
YOUNG GUNS 2 - SMOKE & MIRRORS
YOUNG GUNS 3 - BEYOND LIMITS
YOUNG GUNS 4 - RYKER'S RAIDERS
YOUNG GUNS 5 - ULTIMATE TRAINING
YOUNG GUNS 6 - CONTRACT TO KILL
YOUNG GUNS 7 - FIRST LOVE
YOUNG GUNS 8 - THE END OF THE BEGINNING

A Tanner Series in order

TANNER: YEAR ONE
TANNER: YEAR TWO
TANNER: YEAR THREE
TANNER: YEAR FOUR
TANNER: YEAR FIVE

The TAKEN! Series in order

TAKEN! - LOVE CONQUERS ALL - Book 1
TAKEN! - SECRETS & LIES - Book 2
TAKEN! - STALKER - Book 3
TAKEN! - BREAKOUT! - Book 4
TAKEN! - THE THIRTY-NINE - Book 5
TAKEN! - KIDNAPPING THE DEVIL - Book 6
TAKEN! - HIT SQUAD - Book 7
TAKEN! - MASQUERADE - Book 8

TAKEN! - SERIOUS BUSINESS - Book 9

TAKEN! - THE COUPLE THAT SLAYS TOGETHER - Book 10

TAKEN! - PUT ASUNDER - Book 11

TAKEN! - LIKE BOND, ONLY BETTER - Book 12

TAKEN! - MEDIEVAL - Book 13

TAKEN! - RISEN! - Book 14

TAKEN! - VACATION - Book 15

TAKEN! - MICHAEL - Book 16

TAKEN! - BEDEVILED - Book 17

TAKEN! - INTENTIONAL ACTS OF VIOLENCE - Book 18

TAKEN! - THE KING OF KILLERS – Book 19

TAKEN! - NO MORE MR. NICE GUY - Book 20 & the Series Finale

The MR. WHITE Series

PAST IMPERFECT - MR. WHITE - Book 1

HUNTED - MR. WHITE - Book 2

The BLUE STEELE Series in order

BLUE STEELE - BOUNTY HUNTER- Book 1

BLUE STEELE - BROKEN- Book 2

BLUE STEELE - VENGEANCE- Book 3

BLUE STEELE - THAT WHICH DOESN'T KILL ME- Book 4

BLUE STEELE - ON THE HUNT- Book 5

BLUE STEELE - PAST SINS - Book 6

BLUE STEELE - DADDY'S GIRL - Book 7 & the Series Finale

The CALIBER DETECTIVE AGENCY Series in order

CALIBER DETECTIVE AGENCY - GENERATIONS- Book 1

CALIBER DETECTIVE AGENCY - TEMPTATION- Book 2

CALIBER DETECTIVE AGENCY - A RANSOM PAID IN BLOOD- Book 3

CALIBER DETECTIVE AGENCY - MISSING- Book 4

CALIBER DETECTIVE AGENCY - DECEPTION- Book 5

CALIBER DETECTIVE AGENCY - CRUCIBLE- Book 6

CALIBER DETECTIVE AGENCY – LEGENDARY - Book 7

CALIBER DETECTIVE AGENCY – WE ARE GATHERED HERE TODAY - Book 8

CALIBER DETECTIVE AGENCY - MEANS, MOTIVE, and OPPORTUNITY - Book 9 & the Series Finale

THE TAKEN!/TANNER Series in order

THE CONTRACT: KILL JESSICA WHITE - Taken!/Tanner - Book 1

UNFINISHED BUSINESS – Taken!/Tanner – Book 2

THE ABDUCTION OF THOMAS LAWSON - Taken!/Tanner – Book 3

PREDATOR - Taken!/Tanner - Book 4

DETECTIVE PIERCE Series in order

MONSTERS - A Detective Pierce Novel - Book 1

DEMONS - A Detective Pierce Novel - Book 2

ANGELS - A Detective Pierce Novel - Book 3

THE OCEAN BEACH ISLAND Series in order

THE MANY AND THE ONE - Book 1

SINS & SECOND CHANES - Book 2

DRY ADULTERY, WET AMBITION - Book 3

OF TONGUE AND PEN - Book 4

ALL GOOD THINGS… - Book 5

LITTLE WHITE SINS - Book 6

THE LIGHT OF DARKNESS - Book 7

STERN ISLAND - Book 8 & the Series Finale

THE REVENGE Series in order

JOHNNY REVENGE - The Revenge Series - Book 1

THE APPOINTMENT KILLER - The Revenge Series - Book 2

AN I FOR AN I - The Revenge Series - Book 3

ALSO

THE EFFECT: Reality is changing!

THE FIX-IT MAN: A Tale of True Love and Revenge

DOUBLE OR NOTHING

PARKER & KNIGHT

REDEMPTION: Someone's taken her

DESOLATION LAKE

TIME TRAVEL TALES & OTHER SHORT STORIES

FIRE WITH FIRE
Copyright © REMINGTON KANE, 2016
YEAR ZERO PUBLISHING

This book is a work of fiction. Names, characters, places and incidents either are products of the author's imagination or are used fictitiously.

Any resemblance to actual events or locales or persons, living or dead, is entirely coincidental.

All rights reserved. Except as permitted under the U.S. Copyright Act of 1976, no part of this publication may be reproduced, distributed or transmitted in any form or by any means, or stored in a database or retrieval system, without the prior written permission of the publisher.

 Created with Vellum

Printed in Great Britain
by Amazon

60481009R00111